# REMEMBER
# REENY

This book is dedicated to my husband, Jim, for taking such an interest in this passion of mine. He spent countless hours listening to my ideas over many years while writing this novel. I thank him for his continued support and suggestions and thank him for helping me bring this dream of mine, and his, to a conclusion.

Also

To my sons, Chris and Shawn, and last but not least, my grandson, Dylan, with love.

# A NOTE FROM THE AUTHOR

While this is a work of fiction, a novel, it is based on factual events that took place in history between 1937 to 1947. The names of the characters, locations of events and timing of the story is purely an adaptation of how I perceived things could have taken place.

# Remember Reeny

By

C. F. Bellis

A Novel

# Prelude

It was Mom's eightieth birthday. The regular crowd gathered for her annual celebration. That included me, of course, and her younger sisters, Grace and Shirley, referred to as "the girls," and their daughters, my cousins, Mom's nieces. Altogether, there were eight of us ranging in age from forty to eighty, and we met at Mom's favorite restaurant, The Madison Hotel, for lunch. The birthday party would continue at Grace's house where we would have cake, ice cream, and coffee. This had been our routine every February for the last five years. The unspoken thought this year was, how many more birthdays would she have left.

It was an unusually cold winter day in Western Pennsylvania. I drove the twelve miles to Mom and Dad's house to pick her up worried about the weather and the icy roads. When I got there, she was fussing over Dad, as she always did, making sure he had lunch before we left. The refrigerator, stocked with vanilla ice cream, Hershey bars, and butterscotch pudding would satisfy his sweet tooth for the afternoon. As I walked in the front door, Mom said, "Do I look all right?" She had on a blue blazer. The red chiffon scarf around her neck fastened in the middle with a gold circle pin complemented the jacket. She tugged on the lapels trying to close the jacket over her well-endowed chest and stated, "A blazer like this can cover-up a multitude of sins." I told her she looked great.

Once Mom reassured Dad she would be home before dark, he kissed her on the cheek while rubbing her neck and said, "Have a good time."

The routine was pretty much the same this year as it was the past four years except...Mom had a harder time getting her coat on. Her left arm would not bend in the right direction to go into the sleeve. With a little coaxing and twisting, her hand finally poked out of the cuff. It was more difficult for her to get in and out of the car than last year, but I just blamed it on the weather.

As we were walking from the parking lot to the entrance of The Madison, arm in arm, the wind picked up, and the snow whirled around us like an icy tornado. It was bitterly cold; the wind chill must have been zero degrees. Sheltering ourselves with our arms against the elements, we finally made it inside after struggling to pull the heavy door open against the brutal wind. We were the first to arrive so there was time to situate ourselves and sit down before everyone else got there. Her coat came off a lot easier than it was to put on.

All the booths in the restaurant seated four people, all except one. This one had an accordion like divider that folded into a recess in the wall. The transformed space could accommodate up to ten people. Knotty pine paneling went half way up the back wall of the booth. Wallpaper with mauve colored roses creeping to the ceiling on green vines completed the backdrop. Two tiffany-style swag lights connected by an antique gold chain lit the area with a pleasing amber glow. This was Mom's favorite spot, and this is where we sat. Mom chose the seat at the end of the booth and I sat to her left, aware of the weakness on her left side. She said, "Are you sure I look all right?" while perfectly reapplying her ruby red lipstick with her right hand. It always amazed me how she could do that without looking in a mirror.

I looked at her glowing in the warm light and said, "You look beautiful," and she did.

The group straggled in and with a lot of hugs and kisses and birthday wishes; her party began. The relatives showered Mom with gifts and cards and it was obvious they each had their own connection with her in some way over the years and loved her very much.

Our waitress took drink orders while handing out large plastic-coated menus, amidst the chatter. The gin and tonics, and vodka and tonics, in tall glasses came quickly. I noticed Mom having trouble with her lime; I helped.

The menus were not necessary because we ordered the same thing every year, wedding soup and grilled chicken salads. Our server soon brought the food and another round of drinks.

Mom was struggling to open the cracker packet for her soup. She tried hard, so no one would notice, but I did, and I helped. After lunch, the checks were paid, and we proceeded to Grace's house for the grand finale.

Everyone was getting up to go, but Mom could not move as fast as the others could, so I told them to go on ahead. After going through the familiar struggle with her coat, we made our way to the door. It was then that I realized something was wrong. It was something worse than having a weak left side and natural aging. Mom started walking in a small circle, her feet moving in short jerky steps, unable to stop. She didn't stop until I said, "Mom, Mom, let's go this way," and I motioned toward the door. I took her arm and guided her out the door into the cold and to the car. She didn't let on that anything out of the ordinary had happened and neither did I.

The rest of the afternoon was wonderful. The eight of us sat in Grace's sunroom feeling warm and cozy while looking through the floor to ceiling windows at the snow blowing around the flowerless rhododendrons outside. We talked and laughed for hours telling stories about children and grandchildren, about jobs and lost jobs, and about family history, some of which only Mom knew. Late afternoon came too quick. It was time to go if Mom was going to be home before dark as promised. I gathered up the cards and gifts and a piece of cake for Dad. "The girls" helped Mom with her coat, to my relief. No one mentioned Mom's physical condition, but by the end of the day, everyone at the party knew that she was failing.

Her eighty-first birthday came and went much differently than the previous five. We celebrated this milestone at the nursing home where she had been living for seven months. The regular crowd didn't gather as in years past but some of them did. There was cake and good conversation but sadness in the air.

Everything changed about a month after the last party at The Madison Hotel. I got the call at work. Mom fell, and they think she broke her hip. I left work in a flurry and rushed to Blakely Memorial Hospital to find Shirley sitting with Dad in the emergency waiting room.

A weary looking nurse escorted me back a hallway through a maze of right and left turns, and eventually to Mom lying on a hospital bed hooked up to monitors in a curtained off area. She was amazing, as usual, trying to be cheerful and saying there was no pain.

Mom told me how she fell. She was just sitting on the couch and Dad brought her a bowl of Quaker Oats for breakfast. He made them every morning for the two of them and usually added bananas. She needed more sugar and as she tried to get up to get it, she fell; the bowl, the oatmeal, and she went flying. She landed on the carpet and said, "Now I've done it." The fall was not very hard, but it was hard enough to break a hip, her left hip.

Shirley took Dad home; he had about all he could take for an eighty-one-year-old man. I stayed with Mom at the hospital until the doctor told us what was to happen next. The doctor explained the hip replacement surgery procedure, which would take place the next day. I told Mom I would be back while she had the surgery, kissed her goodnight, and went home. After calling my two sisters and my brother to let them know what happened, I reported myself off work and sat down and cried.

My sisters, who loved Mom as much as I did, came home to help me deal with it all. Cheryl and her husband drove down from Erie and my sister Kate, took a leave from her teaching job in Virginia and made the eight-hour drive to spend time with mom and dad.

Mom went through all the physical therapies there were, and in the end, she still could barely walk and was diagnosed with a disease called Parkinson's Plus. The experts explained her condition as a progressive degeneration of the brain that prohibited signals from the brain to go to the rest of the body. The disease did not respond to Parkinson's type treatments. Her frail body shook uncontrollably with tremor and her left side was basically paralyzed. She was scared to death of falling again. Mentally, she was pretty sharp.

We had many conversations about the fall. She relived the accident a thousand times. More than once, she said, "Why did I have to turn 80?" Mom didn't want to blame Dad for the fall, but she insinuated it more than once because he gave her the oatmeal that morning.

After attempting home care with the help of visiting nurses and all the medical equipment Medicare would provide, we finally accepted the fact; the family could not do it. It took many conversations and tears to come to that realization. All recommendations were, she should be in a nursing home. Her condition required more care that we could manage. Therefore, off she went to The Shawville Medical

Center, the local old age home against her wishes. It broke my heart sending Mom there because I used to work there and vowed I would never see my parents in that place.

Once the situation seemed to be under control, my sisters had to go back to their homes and lives. Then my brother and his wife stepped up and offered to move in with Dad to help care for him. They had the awesome job of cleaning and reorganizing the house to accommodate their things. Week after week, there would be boxes loaded with things for me to take. I brought the boxes home and sorted through them. There were many childhood memories in those boxes, as well as photographs, mail, papers and junk. I cried and laughed as I went through them and threw away the junk. One day, I opened one of the boxes and in it was an old leather handbag filled with letters. I couldn't read them at first, I knew what they were, they were just too personal, and they were Mom's. When we were kids, my sisters and I found the same letters in the attic. I stashed the bag behind my couch and forgot about it for a while.

Eventually I pulled the purse from behind the couch, brushed off the dust, and took a good look at it. It was a large brown satchel with two short tattered straps. The sides of the satchel were etched with bears in the wild. The letters were neatly bundled and wrapped in a torn, discolored plastic bag and they were bulging from the broken zipper at the top. I carefully opened the plastic and separated the two stacks.

I read the fragile letters, carefully placing each page back into its aged, crumbling envelope. In them, I discovered a story, a story about the lives of two men who fell in love with the same woman during the same era; the lives of two men that intertwined through tragic world events and the happiness one woman gave to both of them. This is that story...

# Chapter 1

5/5/1943

Dear Sweetheart,

    I got here 9 1/2 hours after leaving Blakely. I had a long ride. I do not know if I will be here very long. I did not get my clothing yet. We have been taking tests and marching. I'm with the rest of the boys from Shawville. I'm sure glad of that. This sure is a big place, but too big to suit me. We are going to get our suits this afternoon and I think we will be leaving the last of this week, but I don't know where we will go until we get there. I will send you the address when I find out and you can write to me.

    I wish I could get a furlough right now. I sure would go home in a hurry. We have to do everything just right and make our own beds. I don't like it at all.

So long, honey. Until I hear from you or see you. With loads of love and kisses to my darling wife. If I could only kiss you.

Best of love,<br>
honey,<br>
Merle<br>
XXXXXXX

Irene clutched the little postcard with the return address of Fort Meade, Maryland, to her chest resisting the urge to cry, but she did cry as she prayed for Merle and all the other boys who left Blakely just a few days ago to fight the war. Irene wished things were as they were before, before Pearl Harbor and the war. That night she lay in bed alone and eventually she drifted off to sleep, dreaming of the happier days in her young life…

It was the day before Christmas at the Taft homestead. The live tree standing in the living room stood tall in the back yard just yesterday. Irene's dad, Frank, got the axe from the hook behind the door of the shed and with a few good swings; the old pine was on the ground. Even though Irene's mom, Margaret, was nine months pregnant and due any day, she decorated the tree, with Irene's help, started to bake homemade bread for dinner and cinnamon rolls for Christmas morning.

Little Grace was playing in the yard making snow angels when Irene came out to watch over her, so their mom could finish her baking. Grace was just two years old and this Christmas was going to be very special for her. She was anxious for Santa to come and the rest of the family was just as excited because it has been a long time since there was a little one to pretend with.

Irene was sixteen years old and had developed into quite a beauty. It seemed like it happened overnight. She transformed from a tall, skinny, gawky adolescent to a sexy, voluptuous young woman full of adventurous dreams and high hopes. Her short pixie haircut was a thing of the past, now replaced with long shiny black tresses that hung down her back in loose curls. Irene inherited her German good looks from her dad and her dark brown penetrating eyes too. Her defined facial features only made her more beautiful especially when she laughed.

Frank Taft came from a large family. He had eight brothers and three sisters and they all lived within a few miles of each other. Frank was by far the best looking of the dozen. He was tall and thin with a square statuesque build. He stood well over six feet and was extremely handsome. Even though he was forty-five years old, you would never suspect by looking at him. Irene and her dad both had February birthdays, and every year since she could remember, her dad would circle their birthdays on the calendar along with Lincoln's and Washington's and say, "Reeny, only really important people are born in February." This always made her happy. She loved him.

The only noticeable characteristics she inherited from her mother were her fiery Irish temper and her devout Catholic faith.

Margaret Taft was born in 1900 in West Virginia as Margaret McGrady. She had an older sister and two older brothers. By the time, she was ten years old, her parents and two brothers were dead. She lived with her older sister, Shirley, in Western Pennsylvania. Shirley was engaged to be married and had converted to Catholicism for her fiancé, thus Margaret also became Catholic and the two were staunch believers. When Margaret was eleven years old, Shirley got sick and was confined to Our Lady of the Woods, a Catholic Hospital for the terminally ill. Having no other family, Margaret went to live at The Sisters of Mercy Orphanage in Pittsburgh. Shirley died in 1912 leaving Margaret truly an orphan at the age of twelve. The only belongings Shirley had at Our Lady of the Woods were a hairbrush, comb, and mirror set, and a pair of gold rosary beads that were gifts from her fiancé. The priest that officiated at Shirley's funeral mass sent these few items to Margaret along with a letter of condolences. The letter gave details of the funeral and location of her grave, the same cemetery where the rest of Margaret's family was buried.

When Margaret was fourteen years old, a family came to the orphanage looking for a young girl to adopt, mainly to help them care for their own young children and Margaret was just what they were looking for. She was young, religious, and hardworking. Coincidentally, their last name was also McGrady.

The McGrady family treated her good and Margaret was happy there until she met Frank Taft at the St. Joseph's church picnic. He swept her off her feet. Even though he was eight years older than she was, they were married when she was seventeen and he was twenty-five.

Irene tried to find out more about her mother's family, but Margaret refused to talk about them. The hairbrush, comb, and mirror were long gone but the gold rosary beads were never too far from Margaret's reach.

Irene was smart, even though she only had an eighth-grade education from the local one-room school. Irene would have to go to high school six miles away in Blakely to complete her schooling, but her mother would not have it. She told Irene, "It would be too far for you to walk to catch a ride." Irene didn't mind the walk; she wanted to go. As a final resort, Irene tried to convince her mom to allow her to go to the convent with her cousin, so she could continue her education, become a nun, and devote her life entirely to serving Jesus Christ. Margaret said no, and Margaret usually got her way. This time was no exception.

The sound of squeaking oil wells pumping in rhythm echoed in the distance. Irene's brothers, Vince and Eddie were down at the wells with their dad. There were three oil wells on the homestead and they all had names, Well Number 1, Well Number 2, and The Other Well. The oil wells were the lifeline of the family. They provided fuel, heat, electricity, as well as a place for the men to hang out and sample their moonshine where the women couldn't see them. The men from the surrounding farms spent a lot of their time at the wells talking about politics and the impending war. It seemed another world war was on the brink, even though everyone was against it. The country was still recovering from World War I.

The Taft's, like everyone else in the area kept in touch with local, national and world events by listening to the radio. Every night after dinner, they turned on the radio and the family gathered around taking in every word. The radio announcer reported of aggressive acts taking place by Italy,

Japan, and Germany. Earlier in the month, President Roosevelt warned Americans that unless nations acted positively to preserve world peace, armed conflict anywhere in the world would affect all nations.

Just a few weeks ago, on December 12, Japanese bombers attacked and sank the American gunboat, *Panay*, on the Yangtze River in China. Two Americans died. Margaret and Frank paid close attention; they did have two sons who might have to go if the United States got too involved with what was going on over there.

Even though it was Christmas Eve, the wells required attention. If anyone could keep the wells running, it was Frank Taft. He was the best well man around and everybody knew it. Today they were working on the head well, Number 1. Frank said," Eddie, climb up to the top and pull the rods." Eddie, only eleven years old, was scared to death, but wouldn't say he couldn't do it. His older brother Vince was watching, reliving the first time he had to do the same thing. Eddie mustered up all the courage he had, and he did the job. He almost fell and vowed he would never do that again.

Back up at the house, Irene was chasing Grace around the white washed trees in the front yard when she became more interested in the young man that was walking up the lane. The closer he got, the more excited she became. Yes, it was her boyfriend, Merle Heasley. It was a long walk from the Heasley farm to the Taft farm, but he undertook that trek many times to see her. Merle was a couple of years older than Irene, about the same age as Vince, so at first it seemed that his frequent visits to the homestead were to see his friend Vince, but it soon became obvious, he was more interested in his sister.

Irene was not at all interested in boys until her cousin, Milly, started to date a guy. Irene and Milly were best friends, doing everything together until Milly started paying more attention to her new boyfriend than to Irene. Irene's Mom allowed her to walk to the dance hall with Milly, it was just down the road, and a great place for young people to go on Saturday nights.

After feeling left out one night at the dance, Reeny approached Milly and asked, "Why did you ignore me all night?"

"I'm sorry Reeny, but I really like that boy I was dancing with. His name is Morris."

Reeny said, "Okay, you can go to the dance with him from now on and I will just stay home."

"Well, he has a real cute little brother that he is trying to fix up." Milly said. "Do you want to meet him? I told Morris that I could find his brother a date for next Saturday. How about it Reeny?"

Irene thought about it for a while and eventually said, "Sure, why not." She met Merle the following Saturday and they hit it off.

Merle was tall, good-looking, and funny. He wasn't what you would call handsome, but with his blond hair and green eyes, he was not too hard to look at. Merle didn't like school much and after finishing eighth grade, he was glad to get out, unlike Irene. He told his mother, "Schoolin' ain't for me; I want to get a job and make some money." There weren't too many jobs around for an uneducated fourteen-year-old, so Merle spent the next few years helping his dad on the farm and working on old cars for cash.

Margaret was looking out of the kitchen window when Merle plopped down on the snow-covered bank and threw a snowball that hit Irene's arm.  Margaret thought to herself, he always shows up right at suppertime.  Grace jumped on Merle to play.  Irene was getting ready to retaliate for the snowball with one of her own aimed right at his belly when her mom hollered from the window, "Bring Grace in now, dinner's almost ready.  Merle are you hungry?"  Irene threw the snowball anyway and missed him all together.  Laughing, the three of them raced toward the house.

Frank and the boys were walking up the lane, all three knowing they had better be home on time for supper or suffer Margaret's wrath.  Eddie looking a little shaken, ran ahead to tell his mom about his scary ordeal down at the well.  Frank, Vince, and Eddie cleaned up and they all sat down to eat.  Margaret made roast chicken, mashed potatoes, green beans from the garden, and of course homemade bread.  For dessert, they had fresh apple pie.  While they were eating, the smell of cinnamon rolls penetrated the kitchen.

After dinner and dishes, Irene and Merle got a chance to get away alone for a little while.  They took a walk down the path to Well Number 2 and it was there he took her in his arms and they kissed for the first time.  Irene closed her eyes as his lips came closer to hers and when their lips touched she held on to him tight because she felt light headed and dizzy.  When she opened her eyes and looked into his eyes, she knew something special had just happened to her.  It was a feeling she never had before, and it felt good.  "We have to get back before Mom and Dad come looking for us."  She said turning away from him.  Merle walked her back to the house holding her hand and reluctantly went home.

Christmas day came and went with all the usual events at the homestead. Grace woke up at the crack of dawn and toddled down the stairs. She spotted the rag doll under the tree right away and said, "Well, here's my doll." Margaret and Irene smiled at each other quite satisfied with their efforts. Irene got a new dress her mother made, and the boys got new gloves and hats she knitted. After the morning fun, the Taft family, dressed in their finest, Irene in her new dress, went to Mass at St. Joseph's Catholic Church. It was a hectic day for their family, but a typical Christmas and they wouldn't have had it any other way. After Mass, they came home, and Margaret and Irene went about preparing the Christmas meal while the men went to check on The Other Well. Throughout the day relatives and friends visited, and Merle too. Milly and Morris were there too and the four of them enjoyed the day talking, laughing and flirting.

Margaret was exhausted when the day ended. After all the company left and the kids went to bed, Frank helped Margaret climb the stairs to their second-floor bedroom and they lay down together. Margaret thought to herself, the baby is coming soon. Shortly after midnight, Margaret knew she was right. She was in labor. She nudged Frank with her elbow, "Frank, call Dr. Young, it is time." It was a snowy Christmas night and it took Dr. Young longer than usual to get there, but he arrived around 3:00 a.m. By this time, Margaret's water had broken, and the baby was on its way. During the delivery, young Eddie, who slept in the same room with Vince, heard the baby's cries and said, "Vince, did you hear that? I think the cat is under the porch again."

Reeny couldn't sleep that night after spending most of the evening with Merle. She was lying in bed reliving the stolen moments they managed to have together that day. With all the people around it was tricky, but they did manage to get away for a little while and kissed again after they exchanged Christmas gifts. Merle gave her a heart-shaped gold locket on a chain and said, "You keep a picture of me here close to your heart, so you never forget me." Irene had saved her money from delivering eggs from the farm and bought him a new hunting knife. He was glad to get it since he lost his old one last season.

Irene's bedroom was next to Vince and Eddie's and the walls were thin. Just when her eyelids closed for the last time, she heard a cry. Eyes suddenly wide open; she looked over to check on Grace lying in the crib next to the wall. She was motionless, sleeping sound, clutching her new doll. Irene sat up in bed listening hard and then heard Eddie's remark about the cat. The cry came again, and this time she knew, the baby came. She peeked through the crack of her bedroom door just in time to see Dr. Young going down the stairs with tinsel that fell from the doorway shimmering on the back of his dark grey suit jacket.

The baby was born at 3:45 a.m. on December 26, 1937. It was a girl! They named her Shirley, the same name as Margaret's sister who had that premature death twenty-five years earlier. Everyone adored Shirley from the beginning, especially Grace. Grace loved her new baby sister even more than her new baby doll.

Grace and Shirley Taft were inseparable and the two of them became known as "the girls."

# Chapter 2

Five years went by and Irene was wondering what happened to her high hopes and big dreams. Nothing much had changed since she was sixteen and she grew increasingly discontent. She looked toward Christ for hope that she would find her purpose in life. Inside, she knew there had to be more meaning to her existence. She continued to date Merle, but secretly wished for something more. She did not know exactly what, but at the age of twenty-one, she felt there had to be more to life than living on the farm, taking care of "the girls," delivering eggs and working occasionally at the neighboring farm, cooking and cleaning. She also resented her mother for not allowing her to go on to high school or the convent and their relationship soured. Margaret depended on Irene more and more to baby-sit while she went out with Frank to the local beer gardens, even though Margaret called them "dens of sin." Margaret told her children that she didn't go inside these "dens of sin" but instead waited for Frank in the car. After seeing her mom walking funny and giggling in the kitchen after one of these outings, Irene had her doubts. Vince married his longtime girlfriend and they were expecting a baby. Irene was excited for them hoping someday she would have a baby too. Margaret allowed Eddie to go on to high school and Irene thought it was so unfair. She knew if she weren't "a girl," she would have been permitted to go on to high school. The injustice infuriated her.

Merle was quite happy and content with the way things turned out for him. As soon as the steel mill opened in Blakely, he was one of the first to apply for a job. In January 1940, he started work. In order to work in Blakely, you needed to have a ride or have a car to get there and that was no problem for him. He loved to work on cars and he could make any old clunker run. His cherished '37 Ford got him to and from work every day. He also loved Irene with all of his heart and wanted to marry her. Saturday nights were the most fun for Irene. This was when they would drive to Shawville for a night out on the town. The women and children would go to bingo in the Towne Hall while the men would wait for them at one of the beer gardens in town. Margaret loved to play bingo and was lucky too, while Irene just tolerated the caller shouting out B-6 and G-54 just so she could go to the beer garden later. Even though Margaret didn't like the idea of the men drinking in one of those "dens of sin" she minded it less on bingo night.

Shawville was a small town only six miles from the farm. The town originated in the 1800's during the oil boom. There was a time when the population soared, and oil wells dotted the entire landscape. The main street was a red brick hill that went straight up for a mile. There was a hotel, movie theater, grocery store, drug store, a whip factory, seven churches of various denominations, and just as many beer gardens as churches.

One Saturday night in May of 1941, Frank drove Margaret, Merle, Irene, and "the girls" to Shawville, parked his Ford along the red brick hill, and they unloaded. From there the men walked to Mrs. Carlotta's and the women and children walked to the Towne Hall.

Mrs. Carlotta's was the most popular beer garden in town and the nicest. It was a family place where the men would sit around the U-shaped bar and drown their sorrows or celebrate good times with a shot and a beer. The shot was always some rotgut cheap whiskey, whatever Carlotta's had on hand, it didn't matter what, and the beer was always Iron City. At the same time, the women and children could relax and catch up on the local gossip in the back room. A floor to ceiling wall separated the back room from the bar. The only opening between them was a short swinging double door that looked like it came from an old western movie. Red checked tablecloths covered the twenty or so square tables in the backroom, and every table had four wooden chairs and a lit candle in the middle. The food was good and the jukebox flashing in the corner was seldom silent, especially on Friday and Saturday nights.

On this Saturday night, Mrs. Carlotta was tending bar. She usually didn't work on Saturdays but tonight was a special occasion. She was a short, grey haired woman, looking older than her age, even though no one really knew how old she was. They did know her parents came across from Italy in the late 1800's and entered the United States at Ellis Island. Tonight, the main topic of conversation at the bar was the war raging in Europe. Some were for United States involvement, but most were not. Mrs. Carlotta was just glad she lived in Shawville, Pennsylvania right now instead of Italy.

When Frank and Merle entered the bar, they found it crowded, loud and smoky, just the way they liked it. "Roll out the barrel, we'll have a barrel of fun" was blaring from the jukebox as they strode through the swinging doors. They straddled the last two empty bar stools and ordered shots and beers. Frank asked the fellow next to him, "What's the occasion, why is this joint so crowded tonight?"

"It's Ross Kepple's twenty-first surprise birthday party," he shouted back in disbelief, as though everybody would have known that.

Frank smiled, nodded, lit up a cigarette, and then said, "Who's Ross Kepple?"

"You don't know Ross Kepple?" the fellow asked. "He's the best basketball player that ever graduated from Shawville High School. He put Shawville on the map back in '38 when they won the championship. He's on leave from the Navy this weekend so the whole town wanted to surprise him on his birthday."

A few hours and more than a few drinks later, Merle peeked over the top of the swinging doors to see Margaret, Irene, Grace, and Shirley sitting at one of the four-sided tables with their own drinks talking about how Margaret won the twenty-dollar jackpot on the coverall. He started through the doors to join them when he swayed a little. He tried to walk carefully hoping Irene wouldn't notice the slight stagger in his step. Irene did notice his staggering right away and her nostrils began to flare like they did when she was angry, an uncontrollable reflex she inherited from her dad. Margaret looked at her daughter and knew all hell was about to break loose it she did not intervene. "Reeny, don't go and ruin this evening by fighting with Merle."

Irene glared at her mom and said, "I'm not going to sit here and be embarrassed by him again."

Margaret pleaded with her to rise above her anger and get through the night. Irene got the message and tried to compose herself. She thought she loved Merle, since they have been together for almost five years, and she still got dizzy when they kissed, and he could be very nice, but she really hated it when he drank too much and made a fool of himself.

By now, women and children filled the back room and the bar was just as packed with men waiting for Ross Kepple to show up. Ross's brother, Jim, came running in the door shouting, "Here he comes, get ready." Irene looked away from Merle, now leaning on their table to steady himself, and saw a tall young man wearing a white navy uniform, cap and all, coming through the door and as he did the whole crowd, burst into song. "Happy Birthday to you, happy birthday to you, happy birthday dear Ross, happy birthday to you." Then loud applause echoed from every corner of Mrs. Carlotta's place. Only when they started singing, "May you live to be one hundred," did she take her eyes off the handsome stranger in white and look around the room. It seemed everyone in the room was proud to be part of his surprise birthday party, everyone except Merle. He had a look of rage on his drunken face, the look Irene had seen before and dreaded. Trying to avoid a scene, Irene smiled looking up at him and said, "Merle, what's the matter, come and sit with us for a while," and she pulled another chair up to their table. Merle grudgingly sat down between Irene and Margaret, but he wanted to follow the sailor back into the bar to see what the big fuss was about. Eventually that is where he ended up, drinking more and becoming more and more obnoxious.

This was the biggest crowd Mrs. Carlotta has ever had on a Saturday night with practically the whole town of Shawville there at one time or another. The jukebox played non-stop and there was a lot of singing and dancing. Grace and Shirley were dancing too, right in the middle of the floor. Ross was twirling his partner to Glen Miller's, "Pennsylvania 6-5,000," his bell-bottomed trousers flapping with each step. On their final spin, they almost knocked Grace and Shirley over. Taking the two little girls by the hand, Ross danced them back to their table and then took special notice of their older sister who was just about ready to run out and rescue them. He came closer to her and said, "Are these yours?"

"Yes, well no, I mean, they are my little sisters." Irene explained. Margaret took control of the moment and thanked the sailor for bringing "the girls" back to their table.

Ross turned to walk away but hesitated and said to Irene, "Would you like to dance with me?"

Breathing hard and trying to hide it, Irene said, "No I can't, I'm here with someone else." It was then she noticed his pale blue eyes, the color of the sky. Ross apologized and backed up, smiling at her; he couldn't tear himself away. Margaret did not miss a smidgen of what just went on but pretended to Irene that she didn't notice a thing.

Margaret drove the Ford home because Frank had a few too many drinks and so did Merle. Grace and Shirley fell asleep as soon as they got in the car and so did Merle. On the way home, Irene couldn't stop thinking about the popular sailor whose twenty-first birthday they just celebrated. She thought, just who is this Ross Kepple anyway?

# Chapter 3

Shawville High School had the best basketball team ever in the 1937–38 school year. Ross Kepple was seventeen years old and a senior and the greatest player the school had ever had. He had high score at every game with at least ten points and was captain of the Shawville Blue Devils Team.

It was December 1937 and the school were on break for Christmas, but that didn't stop Ross from finding a way to play basketball. The only basketball hoop he could use was in a parking lot in the middle of town. Earlier in the week, a huge snowstorm blew across the area and blanketed Shawville with a covering of white, just what most people wanted at Christmas, except for Ross. Now he had to shovel off the basketball court and soak up the water with old newspapers before he could play. When the court was almost dry, he began to bounce the ball. His mother, Agnes, could see the lot from her kitchen window so it did not surprise her when she heard the rattle of the ball going in the basket. She quickly looked out of the window and smiled. Soon there were six or seven boys from around town playing a game of horse in the parking lot. Even though it was Christmas Eve, the playing went on until dark. It was only then, when they couldn't see the basket anymore; they wished each other a Merry Christmas and headed for their homes.

Ross went home too, to the Central Hotel where he was born in 1920 and where he has lived ever since with his parents, two sisters and his brother. The Hotel sat half way up the red brick hill on the right. His father, William Kepple, moved to Shawville with his wife Agnes from Pittsburgh in 1918, right after their first daughter was born, and bought the hotel. Everyone called him Bill. Ross's parents owned and operated the hotel very profitably until the Great Depression in 1929. After that, life was a struggle. Now the family was poor but happy in the little town of Shawville.

In 1920 when Prohibition became law, the operations of the hotel changed a bit. Now it was illegal to sell liquor at the hotel or anywhere else for that matter. Consequently, the men who visited the hotel spent most of their time in a little storage room behind the bar. The moonshine business is what kept the money flowing during those years for the Kepple family. Prohibition ended in 1933 and since then the hotel bar was busier than ever. However, some old habits were hard to break. The regulars still settled in the storage room and the conversation of the day, besides the high school basketball team, was about politics, President Roosevelt, and the unrest in Europe and Asia.

Ross came inside and entered the living area of the hotel. The smell of homemade chocolate cake penetrated his cold red nose. He was hoping his mom was going to frost it with his favorite, sea foam icing. He peeked into the kitchen and found his expectation had come true. Agnes was stirring and cooking the frosting on top of the stove. It looked like brown bubbling lava about to explode from the top of a volcano. It was just about ready.

Ross matured young, sporting scruffy whiskers by the age of fourteen and his dark bushy eyebrows grew straight across making him look like he had one connected brow. He towered over his parents at six feet, one inch. He had light blue eyes, dark brown hair, and beautiful white teeth. He was a funny guy, always cracking a joke. The girls in his class would giggle and flirt with him but he wasn't interested in them, much. All he really cared about was playing basketball.

Bill was still at the bar trying to get everyone to leave. After all, it was Christmas Eve. Eventually the patrons left, and he made his way into the living room. By now, all the kids were in bed and Agnes was still in the kitchen cleaning up for the next day. Bill sneaked up behind her and kissed her on the neck wrapping his arms around her small waist. He had a few drinks at the bar too. She turned around startled but laughing and said," Bill, get out the presents and put them under the tree."

Christmas Day at the hotel was always exciting. A massive live tree standing in the corner filled the lobby and carols chimed from the Victrola nearby. After opening gifts and going to Mass at the Catholic Church on the top of the hill, the family returned home, and the festivities began. People came from all around to visit, relatives, friends, and some who had nowhere else to go. They were all welcome there.

Agnes was a wonderful cook and she prepared all of her specialties today. Stuffed turkey with all the trimmings, as well as ham, and some polish dishes, favorites of hers from her childhood. There were abundant desserts; chocolate cake with sea foam icing, of course, pumpkin pie, nut rolls, and cookies galore. The guests brought food too, so there was quite a feast. Drinks flowed freely from the hotel bar and soon laughter, music, and fun filled the Kepple home. Everyone sang along to the carols that echoed through the air. Ross was in all of his glory because he was a very good singer. "The Twelve Days of Christmas" was his favorite Christmas song and he took pride in knowing every word.

When the day was over, all Ross could think about was getting back to school after the holiday break and playing basketball. The first half of the season had just ended, and he could not wait to get back into the school gym. Ross looked out of the kitchen window at the tattered basketball hoop in the parking lot before he went to bed and said to himself, tomorrow, tomorrow I will fix the hoop and shoot around.

Soon Christmas recess was over and to Ross's delight school was back in session and the second half of the basketball season was in full swing. The Shawville Blue Devils team was having their best season ever and it looked like they would take the championship. It turned out the regular season for the Blue Devils ended in a tie with Winfield. The tie-breaking game would take place on March 1, at Blakely High School.

The Blakely High School gymnasium was the biggest gym the Blue Devils ever played in. The Shawville High School Band played as the team ran onto the court for pre-game warm ups. Ross spotted his mom, dad, brother, and sisters right away sitting on the bleachers, two rows from the bottom on the right. He dribbled the ball and shot. While trotting to the back of the warm up line, he looked up into the bleachers and saw the largest crowd of spectators he has ever played in front of. The sight was euphoric, and adrenalin rushed through his whole body. The Shawville fans were shouting "Kepple, Kepple, Kepple," in a deafening chant.

The game was about to start but not before the starting quintet got in a huddle. This was the time the captain was supposed to motivate his team with a little pep talk, but before Ross could speak, his co-captain, Ralph McNallen whispered, "Did you see those red shoes Kepple's mom has on?" Trying to keep a straight face, since Coach would kill them if they saw them laughing, the group of five cracked up laughing inside. Ross's face turned as red as her shoes and he couldn't muster up any words of motivation after that.

Kepple was up against Joe Ottolini of Winfield for the jump ball and Ottolini easily out jumped him. Winfield got possession of the ball and was fouled. They made the first bucket of the game as a result putting them ahead 1-0 but the Shawville fans found cause for joy when Holben swished a long shot from the side that gave them a 2-1 lead. After O'Donnell had caged one from the foul line, Holben got his second from the side and Shawville held a 5-1 lead. Callahan dropped through a two pointer as the whistle blew but the timer's desk nullified it when they determined the whistle had blown before he made the hoop. The Shawville fans went wild accusing the timekeeper of cheating but the game went on. Kepple ran the count to seven before Keasey and Ottolini came back with two points to cut the Shawville lead to two points. Kepple and Callahan scored from the field and just before the half, Grelling scored a foul. At the intermission, Shawville sported a five-point 11-6 advantage.

As the second half opened, Keasey scored from the field for Winfield. Kepple however, came back with a field goal, was fouled as he made it, and sunk the free throw. Winfield scored once in two attempts from the foul line and Kepple again scored from the field. Davies added two points for Winfield and as the quarter ended, Kepple was fouled.

Kepple made both fouls as the fourth period opened. Burtner came back with two fouls for Winfield and then Kepple counted again from the field. Grelling's screamer gave the Winfield club new life as they trailed only five points with five minutes of play remaining. Kepple scored from the field again and Keasey countered with a two pointer, Keasey made a foul to approach within four points. With two and a half minutes of play remaining, Callahan got loose and stole the ball from Winfield dribbling down the court, he passed it off to Kepple who shot and scored and was fouled. With ten seconds left in the game, Kepple easily shot the foul. Game over! Shawville won the championship of the Southern Section of the

North Blakely County High School Basketball League, a first for the school.

The Shawville town council organized a parade in honor of the basketball team and people from all around crowded along the main hill as the players walked down toward the honor roll. The student body followed the team carrying banners proclaiming each player's name and the high school band brought up the rear playing the Shawville Alma Mater. The championship and parade were such exciting events in the county, it made the front page of the *Blakely Eagle*.

Now that basketball was over and graduation on the horizon, Ross needed to think about his future. He sure did not want to spend the summer back in the Civilian Conservation Corps in Sligo building fences and pulling gooseberry bushes. That was okay last summer, but he didn't want to do it again, even though the twenty dollars sent to his parents each month helped them survive. The War Department ran the CCC Camps and life there was like being in the military. Ross didn't miss the 5:30 a.m. bugle call that woke him up every morning. If he didn't get up on the first call, the bugler would blow again at 6:00 a.m. He and the other young men in his camp had to line up and march into the mess hall at 7:00 a.m. for breakfast. After breakfast, they would assemble on one edge of the camp's grounds and canvas the entire grounds for rubbish. At 7:55 a.m., each boy got his package of four sandwiches and saved them for lunch. Each crew of twenty-five took two cans of coffee to work also. Ross never drank coffee before but learned to appreciate it now. At 8:00 a.m., they left for their job in a government truck. Ross was assigned to the gooseberry crew.

They canvassed the White Pine Plantation for gooseberry bushes. The crew pulled the bushes out by the roots. The purpose of this was to prevent the blister rust, which gathered on the gooseberries, from spreading to the white pine trees. At noon, the foreman would lecture the crew on subjects like "Safety First," or "How to Fight a Forest Fire." At 4:00 p.m., the crew returned to the barracks and at 5:00 p.m., immediately after roll call, they got supper. After supper, they were on their own to go to the library, or recreation hall. Ross was lucky enough to organize a basketball team at camp and that was his recreation while in Sligo. At 10:00 p.m., the bugler blew taps, which brought silence in the camp. And so, it went day after day.

While Ross was thinking about what to do with his life, his hometown priest, Father Hughes approached him about possibly attending Duquesne University in Pittsburgh on a work-study basketball scholarship. After all he was Catholic, a great basketball player, a pretty-good student and not afraid of work. Father Hughes graduated from Duquesne himself and it just so happened his best friend and former classmate, Dick Davis, was the current men's basketball coach. Using his Catholic influence and a favor from Dick, he succeeded in getting Ross enrolled and on the basketball team. Ross would start in the fall of 1938.

Ross was excited and nervous as he made the trip from Shawville to Pittsburgh that August. His parents took him there along with Father Hughes in their 1936 Ford. Agnes cried as they pulled away from the dormitory where they left their oldest son and she pretended to concentrate of the view from her passenger window, so Bill and Father Hughes couldn't see the tears rolling down her cheeks.

Ross knew he had his work cut out for him with studies and sports ahead of him but was determined to try his hardest. After the first week of classes, the football coach asked him to practice with the team, so Ross took on one more responsibility early in his freshman year. He soon realized that he didn't have enough money to exist in Pittsburgh, even with a basketball scholarship paying his tuition, room and board. Duquesne Gardens, located on the corner of Fifth and Craig Streets, near the college, was hiring ushers for their evening hockey games and Ross got the job.

Ross was very organized and each week he would list in his notebook his work schedule, practice schedules and class schedule. These weekly schedules accounted for every waking moment of his time. He tried as hard as he could to juggle his daily activities but, in the end, was the sixth man on the basketball team and had only a C average, not good enough to get a scholarship for another year. Even though he did not want to, Ross left Pittsburgh and went back to the CCC Camp, this time working in the limestone quarry. This crew chose only the tall healthy men and they became known as the "chain gang." The work was hard and dirty.

Every night after dinner in the mess hall, the radio brought the latest news to the Sligo barracks. The voice of Edward R. Murrow broadcasting directly from London filled the room. Everyone wondered how much longer the United States could stay out of the war that was seemingly out of control in Europe. Over the past few months, the Netherlands fell to the German Nazis as well as Belgium and Norway and German U-boats were attacking merchant ships in the Atlantic. France surrendered to Germany and Britain stood alone. Britain's Chamberlain, who appeased Germany's Hitler, resigned. Winston Churchill succeeded him. Churchill pledged to wage war by sea, land and air with all their might and with all the strength God could give them. He pleaded with Roosevelt for ships to reinforce the British Navy. German planes rained bombs on British cities. They evacuated thousands of children to the north. The British people spent long nights in subway stations below the streets of London to escape the bombs. In an effort to assist Great Britain without committing the United States in the war, President Roosevelt agreed to transfer fifty old but usable destroyers to the British fleet in exchange for a ninety-nine-year lease on naval and air bases in Newfoundland and the Caribbean.

By the end of the summer, Ross knew his days at the Sligo barracks were numbered. The maximum time spent in the CCC Camps was two years and Ross's time was just about up. He thought about trying to get a job at the steel mill in Blakely, but he couldn't afford a car and he didn't even know how to drive. He thought about joining the service, so he could travel the world and maybe see The Great Wall of China, something he has dreamed of seeing since history class in high school. For a poor fellow from small town Pennsylvania, joining the military would be the only way this dream could come true. Ross wasn't sure if enlisting was such a good idea, not right now anyway.

During his latest fireside chat, Roosevelt stated, "American's need not remain neutral in thought." Americans sympathized with Poland, Finland, Britain, and France. Roosevelt tried to repeal restrictions on arms sales to nations at war. Congress fought it. Finally, a compromise called "Cash and Carry" allowed the United States to sell arms to the allies if they paid cash and transported the materials on their own ships. Roosevelt assured the people that there was not the remotest possibility of sending the boys of American mothers to fight on the battlefields of Europe. With Roosevelt's encouraging words in mind, Ross enlisted in the Navy and left Shawville in the fall of 1940. To Ross's surprise, President Roosevelt signed into law the Selective Service Act the week after his enlistment. It was the first peacetime draft ever instituted in the United States. Now, his faith in Roosevelt's encouraging words faltered, but there was no going back now. His six-year contract with the United States Navy was unbreakable.

His dad drove him to Blakely to catch a bus to Pittsburgh and from there he took the train to Philadelphia for boot camp. Ross breezed through it, being athletic and strong. He made many new friends and liked his first six months at the Philadelphia Navy Yard. He even liked the way he looked in uniform, especially the white one.

Ross's assignment was on the USS *Omaha*, and it was on this ship he became a sailor and a smoker. All his peers smoked cigarettes, something he never could afford, but now since he had money coming in from his military pay, he tried it and was quickly hooked.

One routine afternoon in late February, the entire crew heard blaring from the ship's intercom, "Ross Kepple, report topside immediately. Repeat...Ross Kepple, report topside immediately."

His crewmates shouted, "What did you do now Kepple? Boy are you in trouble."

"Nothing, I swear, I don't know what this is about." Ross responded feeling anxiety overtake him. He butted out his cigarette while climbing out of the lower birth of the three high bunks and scurried topside. When he got there, Lieutenant Carmichael handed him a telegram. Ross had never received a telegram in his life. He could only think the worst. Something must have happened to his mother or father or sisters or brother. Terrible thoughts raced through his head.

"Well, open it." Ordered Carmichael.

"Oh, yes sir." Ross said taking a deep breath. He tore open the envelope with shaky hands and began to read;

Coming to Philadelphia...stop...Meet me and Coach at Piccadilly Hotel...stop...Friday, March 3...stop...3:00 p.m....stop...Duquesne playing Ohio State in Philadelphia ...stop...Fr. Hughes...end.

He exhaled a sigh of relief and beamed from ear to ear, practically revealing all thirty-four of his perfect white teeth.

Lieutenant Carmichael said, "It must be good news Kepple."

"Oh yes, yes Sir." Ross said. "Yes, Sir it is." He bounded down the narrow stairwell back down to his bunk realizing for the first time how anxious he was to see someone from home even if it was his local priest and old coach.

He was able to get shore leave on March 3, 1941 and went directly to the Piccadilly Hotel and waited anxiously in the lobby. When he saw Father Hughes and Coach pushing through the revolving door, tears welled up involuntarily in his eyes taking him by surprise. He quickly composed himself and approached them with an outstretched hand. He and Father Hughes enjoyed the game immensely even though his old alma mater lost badly. Since being reunited with them, he couldn't wait to go home; he was suddenly very homesick.

After his promotion to Fireman First Class, he would get a one-month leave. Ross was hoping it fell over his twenty-first birthday, May 18.

Sure enough, Ross's leave began on May 15, 1941. He would be home on his birthday. He wondered if anyone would have a party for him.

# Chapter 4

The day after the party, Ross slept until noon. After all the shots and beers, he had the night before, he could have slept all day. His friends tried to get twenty-one shots down his throat, but Ross lost count after the tenth. He crawled out of bed and headed to the bathroom when he bumped into Jim in the hallway. "Who was that gorgeous brunette at Carlotta's last night?" he mumbled. Jim replied, "Which one, there were about twenty gorgeous brunettes' there last night."

"The one sitting in the back room with the little girls." Ross shouted through the bathroom door.

"Oh, that was Irene Taft, you know the Taft's with the oil wells down on Heist Road." Jim said.

"I never heard of the Taft's down on Heist

Road." Ross said as he stepped out of the bathroom holding his throbbing head with both hands.

"You probably haven't, since you haven't been around Shawville much. You went to the CCC Camp in Sligo, then off to Duquesne in Pittsburgh and now off to the Navy. No wonder you never heard of them, anyway she's dating that Merle Heasley so forget her." Jim said.

Ross thought for a minute and said, "You mean that guy that was so drunk last night he passed out at the bar?"

"That's the one," Jim answered.

Forget her he tried, but Ross could not get Irene Taft out of his mind. The next day he asked his old high school team mate, Ralph McNallen, who had a car to take him to the Taft homestead. Ralph said he knew where the Taft farm was but didn't know if he could get away. Ralph got married right out of high school to his high school sweetheart, Rose Graham, and he worked at The Mill in Blakely. They were expecting a baby and Rose was having a troubled pregnancy. Ross coaxed him to try to get away. Ralph was able to get his mother to stay with Rose for a while. He picked Ross up at the hotel around noon. "You owe me one Kepple. I only have one hour for this wild goose chase and then I have to be back home."

"Thanks Ralph, I promise we will be back in less than an hour." Ross said. After about twenty minutes, they could see the tops of the oil wells and soon the house was in view. There was someone in the yard, but Ross couldn't tell if it was Irene or not. As they got closer he could see it was not her, no it must be her mother and it looked like she was white washing the trees in the front yard. The trunks of three of the four oaks were white, only part way up. The woman was painting the fourth one as they slowly drove past. She stood up and looked to see who it was. Not many cars came out this way unless they knew somebody that lived nearby but Margaret didn't recognize the car and went back to her task. "Turn around and go back", Ross ordered Ralph.

"I will, I will as soon as I find a place to turn around on this old dirt road." There was a lane straight ahead and Ralph turned his car into it.

In the distance, walking toward them was a dark haired young woman with two little girls skipping along beside her. She was carrying a basket in the crook of her arm and it looked like she was on a mission, and she was. "If only Mom didn't make me white wash that old oak before I left, I wouldn't be running late," Irene grumbled aloud as she made the turn toward the O'Donnell farm. She knew Mrs. O'Donnell baked every afternoon and needed her eggs before now. "Grace, Shirley, there's no time to tarry," Irene said, and they scurried to keep up with her.

"The girls" knew Irene was out of sorts and were trying to cheer her up. Grace said, "Reeny, when we get back home, I bet your boyfriend will be there and you two can kiss some more." Shirley laughed and tugged on her arm looking up at her. Irene shrugged her off and kept on walking, too fast. "Reeny, Reeny," Shirley shouted. "I see that dancing sailor man."

"What dancing sailor man?" Irene said looking down at her.

"The one we saw at Carlotta's." Shirley started jumping up and down, pointing and shouting, "There he is, in that car."

Irene didn't even notice the strange car backing out of the O'Donnell lane until now. She looked up right into the blue eyes of the sailor that she has been wondering about for two days and he was looking out of the passenger window right at her. The basket, now in her hand, began to sway and two of the dozen eggs fell to the ground smashing into a gooey pile of white and yellow. Just then, Mrs. O'Donnell came stomping down the lane shouting, "It's about time you got here with my eggs. I'm going to have a word with your mother about this." Irene threw the basket on the ground, grabbed Grace, and Shirley's hands and kept on walking up the road toward home.

Ross jumped out of the car and ran after her shouting, "Irene stop."

She stopped in the middle of the dirt road and sent "the girls" on their way home, and turned around shouting, "How do you know my name and what do you want?"

He came closer and said, "I can't stop thinking about you, ever since I saw you at Mrs. Carlotta's. I want to see you again. I'm home on leave from the Navy for three more weeks. Can we can get together?"

"I don't know," Irene said, "I told you I'm seeing someone."

"You're not married yet, are you?" asked Ross.

"No," she said.

"I need a partner for the square dance at The Grange on Friday. You do square dance, don't you?" Irene nodded while he continued; "I'll pick you up Friday night at eight."

Before Irene could answer, Ralph pulled up and said, "Get in Kepple, Rosie's going to kill me, this took a lot longer than one hour." Ross quickly gave Irene a kiss on the cheek and leaped into the car and they were gone leaving a cloud of dust in her path.

Irene walked slowly the rest of the way home wondering what had just happened. When she got there, she walked right past her mom and sisters in the yard, straight into the house and up the stairs to her bedroom where she closed the door and locked it behind her, waiting for Mrs. O'Donnell's wrath.

Merle was coming over tonight and Irene did not even care. She didn't know how to feel about him or Ross Kepple who announced he was taking her to a square dance on Friday. For the first time in years, she had a feeling deep inside her of excitement and anticipation. She didn't know where it came from, but it was there, and she liked it. Merle was working the afternoon shift at The Mill this weekend, so maybe she could see Ross Kepple on Friday. No, it would not be right, but she was going to do it anyway, against her better judgement. Irene told her mom about the date and Margaret promised not to tell Frank or Merle. She liked the sailor and secretly wished Irene would find someone better than Merle Heasley to spend the rest of her life with. Irene was free to go.

What would she wear? Irene tried on at least three different dresses before settling on the white one with black polka dots. It had a sweetheart neckline and a fitted bodice that enhanced her shapely figure. The gathered skirt billowed from her small waist and she wore a ruffled petticoat underneath to accentuate the fullness of the skirt. Her mom helped her clip a white bow in the back of her hair to hold the dark tresses in place. Margaret offered Irene her pearl necklace to wear, just this once. Black and white pumps and a matching bag completed the outfit.

Ralph's car pulled up to the house at 7:45 on Friday night and Ross got out of the back seat and walked to the kitchen door. Nervous as a schoolboy, he knocked gently. Irene took one last glance at herself in the hallway mirror, touched up her lipstick, and hurried to the door. His eyes lit up as they devoured the sight in front of him. "Irene, you sure look swell." He said.

Smiling, she turned her head slightly to the left while looking down and said, "Thank you." He took her by the arm directing her to the car. They slid into the back seat and Ross introduced Irene to Ralph and Rosie. Irene and Rosie immediately struck up conversation about Rosie's pregnancy, a conversation Irene had perfected long ago. Margaret and "the girls' peeked out of the second-floor bedroom window with the lights out so they couldn't be seen and watched as the car drove away. The last glimpse they saw was the silhouette of Irene looking at Ross as he put his left arm around her shoulders.

Irene saw Ross as often as she could over the next three weeks, juggling her time between Merle and Ross. Lucky for her, Merle was working all the double shifts The Mill offered, so he wasn't around much.

They went back to Mrs. Carlotta's and it seemed every time they did "Marie" was playing on the jukebox. They danced to it so many times;

it became their song. At the end of each evening, Ross would hold Irene tight and kiss her lips running his fingers along the soft skin of her neck. On the way home one night he said, "Irene, if we ever get married and have a little girl, let us name her Marie."

She wouldn't admit it, but she was falling in love with Ross Kepple. She felt guilty for what she was doing and went to confession every week and on Sundays at Mass she prayed for guidance and direction.

Three weeks passed too quickly and soon Irene was kissing Ross goodbye at the Blakely bus station with tears in her eyes. The bus ride to Pittsburgh was about one-hour long. Then Ross would board the train for Philadelphia. They separated from their last kiss and Ross stepped inside taking a window seat, so he could have one last glimpse of her. He looked frantically for her but couldn't see her anywhere. Another passenger came on board right before the driver closed the door for departure. Ross looked up toward the front of the bus and was ecstatic to see Irene making her way down the aisle toward him. He reached for her smiling, took her in his arms and held her tight. "What are you doing?" he asked while kissing every inch of her face.

"I just can't leave you yet. I bought a round trip bus ticket, so we can be together as long as possible." They spent their last hour together just holding each other and wondering where this would lead. Ross had five more years in the Navy and Irene had Merle. Her head was spinning at what to do. They promised to write to each other and Irene cried as the train bound for Philadelphia pulled away from the station.

Now that Ross was gone, Irene tried to concentrate on Merle. He loved her, and he needed her. She knew it. Ross Kepple had a five-year commitment to the Navy. Who knows when he would be back? It was just a fling and it was over. She decided to try to stick with Merle, he was here, and he was hers.

Then the letter came. The return address was from Philadelphia, Pennsylvania. Who could it be from? The whole family wondered as they waited for Irene to get home. Eddie said, "It's from that guy from Shawville." Nobody else speculated aloud. Merle and Irene walked into the kitchen around 8:00 p.m. Margaret slipped the letter under the doily on the kitchen table. Frank and Merle went down to the Other Well, why, they could only imagine.

As soon as they left, Margaret handed the letter to Irene and said, "What are you going to do?" Irene grabbed the piece of mail addressed to her, looked at her mom, and said, "I don't know." She ran up the stairs and flopped down on her bed ripping open the envelope. Turning up the light on
the wall, she read:

June 25, 1941
USS Omaha
Philadelphia, PA

Dear Irene,
I just wanted you to know I'm thinking about you and wondering how you are. I hope everyone is all right at your place.

Well I found the ship all right. We're anchored in the Philadelphia Bay. In a day or two, we are going to ship out on neutrality patrol. No one is supposed to know where, but I have a feeling it is the Southern Atlantic.

I had such a wonderful time with you when I was home. You were swell. You treated me so nice. I keep thinking how we danced to "Marie." Wasn't it wonderful? I am really happy when I'm with you. I want you to believe what I'm saying. Please don't think I'm giving you a line. I hope you want to see me some more because I know I have to see you. I just have to.

Reeny, we do seem to get along good together, don't we? We never had an argument, did we? I could never do anything to hurt you. I like you too much. I miss you very, very much already.

Remember when you said you were crazy about me. That got me. Did you actually mean it? I know I'm crazy about you Reeny. I'll always think you are swell. Boy, I've really been lonesome since I left you. I was really happier than I ever was every time I was with you. It really made a fellow like me feel so dam good to be treated so nice by such a nice girl. You are tops as far as I'm concerned.

We should be on neutrality patrol for six months. I wish I didn't have five years to go yet in the Navy now that I met you. If I can get any weekends off when we get back from patrol, I'll come home to see you, if you want me to. Of course, I wouldn't want to come if you didn't want me to. Please don't go and get married while I'm away at sea. Just wait until we can see each other again.

I can't wait until I can see you, hold you, and run my fingers along your nice soft neck. Boy I like that honey. I love it.

Lots of Love,<br>Ross

Irene heard the familiar sound of the kitchen screen door squeak open and the voices of Merle and her dad. She quickly stuffed the letter under her pillow and listened. "Frank, I love Irene, and would like to marry her but she won't even talk about it."

Frank replied, "What's the hurry? Give her some time, she'll come around." They both said, "Cheers" as their glasses of moonshine clicked, and they laughed.

The next morning Irene got her writing paper out of her dresser drawer. The paper was her favorite. It was pale pink with clusters of roses in the right-hand corner and roses adorned the inside of the pink envelopes. She hoped they didn't look too girley, but it was all she had.

June 30, 1941
R.D. 2
Shawville, PA

Dear Ross,

I was so happy to hear from you, I was afraid you wouldn't write to me, but now that you did, well, I just feel wonderful. I was really glad you found your dear old ship. Were you glad to see her?

We are all fine here, except Shirley gets the earache once in a while. Yes, we sure did have a wonderful time when you were home. I'll never forget it. You say I was nice to you. Well, you really were nice to me. You made me very happy. I've been thinking of you about every minute since you left. I thought maybe it was only me, but since I got your letter, and you said you were thinking of me too, I feel better. I knew I was going to miss you Ross, but I didn't know I'd miss you as much as I do and I'm sure I'd have died if I didn't get your letter. It really meant a lot to me. You said everything I wanted you to say. You just seem to know how to make me happy. No wonder we get along so swell, and we really do.

Yes, I do want to see you some more. I was afraid you would forget about me, and I didn't want you to forget.

I hope you do get to come home when you get back from patrol, but six months is a long time, you might forget me by then. I sure will be glad to see you again. I miss you so much. That last night, when I left you, I cried the whole way home. I was lonesome the minute you left.

It has been pretty nice here this last week. It's been warm and there was a pretty moon a couple nights ago. So, I looked at the moon and thought of you. But we don't mind cold nights, do we?

Last Friday, Mom and "the girls" and I went in town and we stopped at the hotel. They were having a party for Mom's friend, so I had a couple of beers and listened to "Marie" on the jukebox. Boy I wish you were home because dear I really am crazy about you. Didn't I tell you that I never say things I don't mean? You believed me, didn't you?

Now you will be on patrol in the South Atlantic, you think, for six months. That won't be so long, and I hope you get home for Christmas.

Grace and Shirley said to tell you to hurry home because they want to dance with you. I think I should be jealous, don't you?

Be careful, <u>go to church,</u> and don't forget to think about me. I'll be thinking of you for that's all I ever do. Write.

All my love,
Irene

# Chapter 5

The USS *Omaha*, categorized as a Task Group light cruiser, with a crew of four hundred and eighty-eight sailors left Philadelphia on July 1, 1941 for a six-month patrol in the South Atlantic. Captain Theodore E. Chandler was at the helm and Lieutenant George K. Carmichael was his right-hand man. Destroyers *Jouett* and *Somers* accompanied the *Omaha* and they were looking for German commerce raiders in the neutrality zone. Ross had never been away from harbor for more than a few days, so he was a little anxious about being at sea for six months. He also wondered if he would lose touch with Irene Taft. He hoped not. Ross got his last mail call on shore before the ship left port and there was no letter from Irene. Maybe she didn't get my letter he thought or maybe she just doesn't want me bothering her. "She will probably be married by the time I get back from patrol," he said to himself as he went down to set up his bunk in the bottom of the ship. The first night on the ship he lay in his bed with his eyes closed dreaming about the times he and Irene spent together. He held her in his arms and caressed her soft skin, and then he kissed her luscious lips. He ran his hand through her shiny dark hair. It made him feel good allover. The sway of the ship woke him in the middle of the night and his dream was shattered.

His voyage on the *Omaha* took him to places he never would have seen if it weren't for the Navy. He saw Brazil, Panama, Puerto Rico, and Cuba so far in his Navy career. Ross was still counting on seeing The Great Wall of China before it was all over.

They saw some action in the fall of 1941 and sank the German blockade-runners *Burgenland*, *Rio Grande*, and *Weseland*. They were carrying cargo from Japan to Europe. Rubber tires filled their holds. Ross wrote to his mother, "You could see tires all the way to the horizon, thousands of them."

Another incident called the *Omaha* to action when the Captain was notified that a German submarine torpedoed a Brazilian ship about four hundred miles away. The *Omaha* arrived in time to rescue the Brazilian sailors but were unable to salvage the cargo, coffee.

Month after lonely month went by on board the *Omaha* and while the other sailors got regular mail from their wives and girlfriends, Ross got none. He did get mail from his brother and mother, but that was it, nothing from Irene Taft. He tried to forget her.

Recife, Brazil was the *Omaha*'s destination to refuel after a long three-thousand-mile patrol.

While refueling was taking place, the sailors were able to go on shore for a few hours. Ross took advantage of this time to get some pictures taken of him in uniform. He donned himself in the white one and flashed the best smile he could conjure up. This was the photo he sent back home.

The shore excursion was short, and they were quickly back on patrol. On November 6, 1941, a large ship was visible on the horizon. Was it another German blockade-runner or a friendly ship? It was too early to tell. As the *Omaha* got closer, Captain Chandler could see the American flag flying as well as two American business flags, B.F. Goodrich and General Electric, waving in the wind. All hands took a deep breath. The vessel carried the name *Willmoto* of Philadelphia on her stern. The Captain recorded their coordinates in his logbook, 00 degrees 40'N, 28 degrees 04 degrees W. They were real close to the equator.

Ross was topside when the ship was spotted and just as Captain Chandler gave the clear signal for the *Willmoto* to pass, Ross noticed something was wrong with her. Through his binoculars, he could see the shape of the stern of the ship was flat. Ross knew that no ship built in Philadelphia had that shape having spent some time in the navy yard there. Ross frantically approached Lieutenant Carmichael shouting, "Stop the Captain. That ship is suspicious." After much persuasion, Captain Chandler was convinced to investigate further. He ordered the ship to stop by shooting a shot across *Willmoto*'s bow. This prompted *Willmoto* to take evasive actions. She reversed her engines and came to a stop. Their fears were confirmed when the American Flag was lowered from the looming vessel and one with the German swastika was raised. Lieutenant Carmichael quickly organized a boarding party. He picked only German speaking sailors aboard the *Omaha*. At that moment, Ross was wishing he never took that German class at Duquesne. As well as being a First-Class Fireman, he was one of the first chosen to board the ominous ship. Every member of the boarding party carried a 45-caliber pistol and a navy knife. They took to the lifeboats and immediately hoisted a signal to indicate the ship was sinking. When Ross's lifeboat pulled up alongside the foreign ship, a deafening explosion came from within the hull. Ross heard one of the fleeing men shouting in German, "This is a German ship, and she is sinking." They were able to salvage the vessel and capture the crew. The freighter, as it turned out was the German blockade-runner, *Odenwald*. The *Omaha* took fifty prisoners to Trinidad and then San Juan. On route to Trinidad, some of the *Omaha* crew chipped in and bought the prisoners ice cream. It wasn't how purported prisoners normally were treated, but the Captain allowed it. In appreciation of the kind treatment, the Germans entertained the crew with accordion music, again unusual under the circumstances.

The cargo was three thousand tons of raw rubber valued at one million, five hundred dollars. Due to the Law of the Sea, the *Odenwald* was considered a prize of war. The value would be split among the owner of the ship, the crew of the *Omaha* and the United States government. Ross could possibly receive over a thousand dollars. The news of the capture spread back to the states. Before he could write his family, Ross's mother read about it in the *Pittsburgh Sun-Telegraph*. The article ended with the quote "Ain't it hey?" She cut the article out and mailed it to Ross. They were so proud of their son.

The USS *Omaha* was still patrolling in the South Atlantic on December 7, 1941 when Captain Chandler made an urgent announcement to the crew. "This morning, Japan attacked our fleet at Pearl Harbor. The casualties are unknown but expected to be in the thousands. At the time of the attack, the United States Navy had twenty-six destroyers, five cruisers, and seven battleships stationed there. The damage reports have not come in yet. It is feared that catastrophic damage has been done to the fleet. Men, now is the time to be strong and pray. I will update you on our situation as information comes in." The entire crew somehow felt the *Odenwald* incident had something to do with the beginning of United States involvement in World War II. They knew their lives would never be the same.

# Chapter 6

Irene's letter to Ross was stamped on the outside of the envelope, "Return to Sender, No Such Address." She double-checked the address Ross had given her and was sure she got it right. Regardless of the returned letter, she checked the mailbox every day for news from Ross, but none ever came. The disappointing weeks went by and she could not stop thinking about him, especially how he would feel her neck when they kissed. After many months passed with no news, she thought about him less and less.

Merle was making good money at The Mill and saving up, so he and Irene could get married and get their own place to live. One day in the fall of 1941, Merle proposed to her and gave her a beautiful, brilliant diamond ring he picked out himself. He put the 1/3 carat diamond set in gold on her finger expecting her to be elated. Instead, Irene seemed agitated while saying yes, she would marry him but would not set a date, not yet. This bewildered Merle but did not argue with her remembering what Frank Taft had told him before. She'll come around.

Merle was on a long weekend from The Mill the first Sunday in December and he came over to visit Irene and spend a relaxing afternoon together. It was a crisp winter day. Frank and Margaret went to Vince's house to see their new granddaughter and took "the girls" with them. Eddie was visiting his girlfriend. Irene tuned the radio to the new station that just came on the air from Blakely in September, WOSR. "Pardon me boy, is that the Chattanooga Choo Choo," echoed from the small speaker. Irene sang along and took a hold of Merle by the hands pulling him up off the couch to dance.

"On track twenty-nine," he sang back. They sang and danced to the whole song, well, almost the whole song...

Interrupting the last verse was a breaking news alert. "We are sorry to interrupt this broadcast with the following announcement. Japanese warplanes have bombed the United States Naval Base in Pearl Harbor, Hawaii. President Roosevelt has just announced it is feared thousands are dead and hundreds of United States Navy ships are destroyed or severely damaged." After this shocking news came over the airwaves, Irene's mind started racing. Did they say thousands of dead at a naval base? Could Ross Kepple be one of them?

Merle took her in his arms and hugged her so tight she thought she would stop breathing, bringing her back to reality. He whispered in her ear, "We have to get married right away."

When she could catch her breath, she shook her head refocusing on his words. She looked at Merle and said, "Why, why now, why right away?"

"Why now? You know Roosevelt will declare war on Japan and they will be drafting all of the men they can now to fight the Japs and that will probably include me."

Once she realized what Merle was trying to tell her, they clung to one another both fearing the worst. They got married as soon as they could. The wedding took place at St. Joseph's Church on January 9, 1942. It was the coldest day of the winter. Irene prayed it wasn't an omen. Ross Kepple could no longer be a part of Irene's thoughts or life.

The new Mr. and Mrs. Merle Heasley rented an apartment on Slippery Rock Street in Shawville. Moving to town would be a new experience for both of them since they have lived all of their lives in the country.

They drove up to the house where their second-floor apartment was located. Smiling, Merle looked at Irene and said, "Home sweet home." She laughed, leaned over the gearshift, and kissed him on the cheek. Their '37 Ford was filled with everything they could fit in it, but before unloading, Irene jumped out and ran up the outside stairway leading to her very own kitchen door. There were twelve stairs before coming to a platform landing and then twelve more stairs to the door. Before Merle could close the driver's side door, she was inside her own kitchen and a feeling of happiness and hope overwhelmed her.

Merle came bounding up the stairs carrying a bottle of brandy Frank had slipped to him down at Well Number One the night before the wedding.

"What's that in your hand?" asked Irene running from room to room.

"It's your dad's blackberry brandy, a housewarming gift," Merle said grinning. "Cheers," he said as he popped the cork and took a long drink. He handed the bottle to Irene and she took a taste, her face scrunching up as the tart liquor rolled down her throat.

"Cheers to you too," she remarked. The two hugged each other happy to start this new chapter of their lives. In the back of both of their minds was always the looming fact that Merle could be drafted at any time.

At first living in town was fun. From their apartment, they could walk to the grocery store, the movie theater, and even Mrs. Carlotta's beer garden. Even though Merle frequented Carlotta's often, Irene tried not to go there for it just brought back memories of Glen Miller's, "Pennsylvania 6-5,000" blaring from the jukebox, dancing to "Marie" and of course Ross Kepple. Instead, she entertained herself by going to the movies. Her favorite movie of the time was *Casablanca*. Humphrey Bogart and Ingrid Bergman were brilliant in a romantic war movie that took place Paris and Africa. Irene envisioned herself as Elsa, portrayed by Bergman, hopelessly in love with one man but committed by marriage to another. In her fantasy, Merle was Vincent, her husband in the movie, and Ross Kepple was the charming Rick Blaine, owner of Rick's Café Americain in Morocco, depicted by Humphrey Bogart. Bogart was not nearly as handsome as Ross was, but masculine and sexy in his own rugged way. Elsa was torn between honor and duty or following her heart. When the movie ended, Irene was immersed in her daydream and it took her a few minutes to snap back to reality. The theater was almost empty by the time she gathered her things to leave. She walked home from the theater feeling strangely empty and sad. She could not explain it.

Since the United States declared war on Japan, everything was changing. Hundreds of young boys enlisted in the service and patriotism ran high throughout the country. The news on the radio got worse every day. Germany declared war on the United States and Hitler was overtaking Europe. Japan invaded the Philippines and the entire Pacific was at risk.

Irene and Merle tried to live life as normally as possible trying not to think about the war. He worked at The Mill and she took up housekeeping for the two of them. Merle did not like living in town and since the government started rationing gas, they had to use it wisely. Three dollars' worth of gas a week was all they were allowed. They found a house for rent in the country closer to Blakely and The Mill and they moved. A one lane wooden bridge that creaked every inch of the way across interrupted the dirt road that led to their new home. The bridge was nearly one mile from their house and the subject of many a ghost story. Irene's palms would sweat, and her heart would race every time she had to go over it.

They talked about having a baby, something she wanted very much, and they decided to try harder.

On their first wedding anniversary, Irene wanted to surprise Merle with the good news. Yes, she was expecting and thrilled to death. He was working daylight, so she had all day to prepare his favorite dinner, steak, and potatoes with corn. After taking a long bubble bath and dressing in Merle's favorite dress, a low cut black shift that flattered every curve on her body, she set the table with their good dishes, a wedding gift from her mom and dad, and lit two tall candles. Irene carefully sliced the loaf of bread she bought that afternoon using the sharpest knife in the drawer. She just couldn't believe the government banned sliced bread after all of the sacrifices the country already made. President Roosevelt ordered all metal parts, including bread slicers to go to the war effort. She made sure she didn't cut herself.

Merle would be home at four thirty that afternoon. Irene threw an apron over her dress and put the steaks in the cast iron skillet at four o'clock, so they would be just right when he came through the door. She decided to wait until they ate and then tell him about the baby. Everything was perfect. How-ever, four thirty came and went, the candles burned out, and the steaks got tough and cold. She got worried when several hours passed and there was no Merle. At about seven o'clock car lights flickered through the living room window. Irene jumped up off the couch and ran to the door. It was their Ford and Merle was crawling out from under the steering wheel. He was drunk. When he staggered through the door, Irene started screaming at him with a rage she didn't even know she had. "I was so worried about you and you come home drunk on our wedding anniversary. The dinner I made for you is ruined." Then she began to cry.

Instead of apologizing, he bellowed back, raised his hand, and hit her across the face shouting, "I'm the man of the house, and I can do whatever I want. I don't have to answer to you." Then he kicked her, and she fell to the floor. He unsteadily made his way to the bedroom, fell onto their bed and passed out. Irene pulled herself up from the floor worried about the baby and lay down on the couch sobbing herself to sleep.

The next morning Merle didn't remember much of what had happened the night before but apologized profusely when Irene told him. He was very sorry; he always was after he took a drunken rage. It was then she told him about the baby and he cried for joy and out of shame for what he had done. "I love you Reeny, I'm so sorry, please forgive me. I'll never drink again if you only forgive me." She had heard that before, she forgave him before, and she forgave him now. Irene started having cramps and spotting blood over the next few days. She knew something was wrong. She tried to rest and not exert herself and prayed that everything would be all right.

On February 10, 1943 the postcard from the selective service came. It was a draft notice. Merle had to report to the Blakely Memorial Hospital for a physical examination on February 15. They knew he was bound to be drafted but when it actually happened, Irene and Merle were shocked.

Merle had not had a drink since January, as promised, but when he got his draft notice, he went over the edge. Drink he did, and then he would come home and fight with Irene and beg her to forgive him the next day. One day in March after one of these nights, Irene bled heavily, and she lost the baby. Great sadness took over the Heasley home and no one laughed or barely talked.  Irene blamed Merle for the miscarriage and he blamed himself.

Irene prayed to be able to forgive Merle again, but this time it was harder to do.  Her Catholic faith kept her from falling apart during this time.  She knew divorce was out of the question. He pleaded with her for yet another chance and Irene gave it to him, again.

In April, Merle got his final notice.  He was to report to the Blakely Court House at 7:45 p.m. on May 3, 1943 prepared to leave for camp.  The notice went on to say bring only your toilet articles and a very small supply of clothing, as you will be outfitted upon arrival at camp. Your travel bag should be small.

Merle wasn't the only one called to fight the war.  There were hundreds of young men from all over the county that were to report on the same day.  The drafted boys would leave Blakely by bus to where, nobody knew.  They would find out when they get there.  Well-wishers packed the streets of Blakely huddling underneath umbrellas seeing their loved ones off.  A band played "God Bless America" as they boarded the buses.  Merle's family and friends were there too, and they watched and cried as Irene kissed him goodbye in the rain.

# Chapter 7

Irene turned over in bed to cuddle up to Merle before he had to get up for work, but she soon realized she must have been dreaming because he wasn't there and wouldn't be for a long time. As she got out of bed, the crumpled postcard fell to the floor and the reality of her situation hit her hard. He was in Fort Meade, Maryland waiting to be transported somewhere to be trained to fight the war.

She was now alone in their little house in the country. Her mom and dad wanted her to move back home and stay with them while Merle was gone, but Irene didn't want to. What she really wanted to do was go to where he was. What she had to do is get a job. The fifty dollars a month she would get from the military was not enough to live on. She heard that hundreds of men were drafted and The Mill in Blakely was going to hire women to fill their jobs. Even though her work experience consisted of Mother's Helper and Housewife, she applied. Irene got the call to go to The Mill for tests and a physical. She got the job along with fourteen other women, the first women to work in The Mill.

Irene was apprehensive about her new job. She never had a real job, not one that paid as much as The Mill did. On May 31, 1943, she drove the Ford to Blakely and reported to the front gate of the steel mill. She was sure glad Merle took such good care of it because she needed a reliable ride to work each day now.

The fifteen women were furnished with blue dungaree overalls and hard hats. They were given a punch card for the time clock and shown where their lockers were. The new employees spent most of the day filling out paperwork and waiting around for someone to give them a tour of the plant to explain what they would be doing. The work would be labor intensive, and it was a hot, dangerous, and dirty place.

Then they met their boss. His name was Harry Barron. The minute Irene heard his name she started to feel sick. Merle had told her all about Harry Barron. He worked for Harry for about three months. According to Merle, "It was three months of hell!" Merle's description of him was quite accurate. Barron was short, five feet five inches, maybe. He wasn't fat, but he had a round protruding stomach that drooped over his low-slung belt. He was always chewing on the end of a fat smelly cigar, sometimes lit, sometimes not.

Irene's mind raced to remember what Merle told her about him. Oh yes, he was not very nice to "his people." That was what he called the employees that worked for him. Harry almost fired Merle for showing up late for work a few times, usually after Merle was out late drinking. A few days before Merle got his draft notice, he got a final notice from Harry. "Heasley, if you're late one more time, you are out of here." Merle hated him.

Each of the new employees had to introduce themselves to their boss. As Irene approached him, the stale cigar smell made her feel sicker.

"I'm Irene Heasley," she spurted out and held out her hand.

"Are you related to Merle Heasley?" he asked with a smirk on his face, making no responding effort to greet her.

"Yes, he is my husband." Irene said, lowering her arm and at the same time holding her head up and standing as tall as she could, towering over him.

Harry said nothing back to her, but she heard him whisper to a clerk standing nearby, "I hope she's not as lazy as her old man."

She tried to stay as far away from Harry as she could but sometimes he would come up behind her, reach up, and put his hand on her shoulder and squeeze. He gave her the heebie-jeebies.

Irene stopped by the homestead on her way home from work to look for her locket that Merle gave to her a long time ago. She opened the kitchen door and called "Hoo Hoo, is anybody home?" Grace and Shirley just about suffocated her with hugs and kisses.

"Reeny's here, Reeny's here," they screamed. Margaret and Frank came running from the living room to see what all the commotion was about.

Frank said, "Hi Reeny how was your first day at The Mill?"

"Okay" she said. "Hey Mom, do you know where my gold locket is? I've looked everywhere, and I can't find it."

"No, I haven't seen it. I thought you wore it when you and Merle got married." Margaret replied.

"I did, but I can't find it now. I have an appointment at Hemphill Studio tomorrow night to get my picture taken and I wanted to wear it. I want to send a picture to Merle. You did know he was transferred to Fort Riley in Kansas a few weeks ago." Just then, Shirley produced the locket. She ran to her room and retrieved it before anyone would discover she had it hidden in her dresser drawer.

Even though Grace and Shirley were often referred to as one entity, "the girls," their personalities had developed into two very different children. Grace, now seven years old was reserved and well-mannered while five-year-old Shirley was rambunctious and devilish. Therefore, it would have been no surprise to anyone that Shirley had the locket hidden in her own dresser drawer.

Frank said, "I'm not much of one for writing so tell Merle I am praying for him and thinking of him."

"Sure Dad," Irene said.

"Why don't you stay here tonight? Your old room is still the same." Frank suggested.

"Stay, stay," the girls" screamed.

Her mom nodded, and Irene said, "Okay, It's a little lonely at home."

The following day after work, Irene arrived at the photography studio looking disheveled. She tried to pull herself together, patting down her windblown hair and touching up her lipstick. She went into the dressing room and changed from her high-collared ruffled white blouse to a black V-necked drape. One quick look in the mirror reflected her transformed appearance. The drape accentuated her full bosom and long neck. The sparkling gold locket fell in just the right place on her chest. She stepped out of the dressing room and Mr. Hemphill's wife handed her a gold tube. "Irene, try this lipstick, it's the latest shade of red."

During the photo shoot, the photographer exclaimed, "I never knew Jane Mansfield had a twin sister." Irene blushed at the compliment and laughed. The camera flashed. She sent that image to Merle in Kansas.

June 7, 1943
R.D. 2
Shawville, PA

Dearest Merle,

How are you darling? I am fine, and I hope you are too. I'm writing this at work, so I need to hurry and finish before old Harry Barron shows up snooping around. You were sure right about him. No wonder you didn't like him.

The Ford is running pretty good but it rattles a lot. It needs you to fix it up I guess. I surely wish you were here. I'm feeling pretty awful without you.

I am sending you the picture of me that you asked for. I hope you like it. Be sure and take good care of it.

I got two letters from you today honey and was I glad for I surely like them. I wish you were home my sweetheart. I do.

Well, I will close for now. Everyone is fine here. I will write you a long letter tonight. Good-bye now honey. I love you and hope you love me dear.

Your Wife,
Irene
XXXXXXXXXXX

P.S. Are you being a good boy for me?

Irene gave her lips a thick coat of red lipstick and purposely kissed the letter. A kiss for Merle she thought to herself. She creased the stationary neatly around her photograph and tucked them into the envelope just in time. Harry Barron walked into the room. "Hello Harry," she said too quickly.

"Hello Irene," he responded, and a reeking circle of smoke penetrated the air. "You know, you have lipstick all over your face, clean up. I can't have my people looking like that," and he grumbled out of the room to make someone else miserable. She hated him too. If she didn't need the money so desperately, she would have walked out at that moment.

June 14, 1943
Fort Riley, KS

My Darling Wife,
How is my pet by this time? I hope well. I'm okay, but a little tired. I suppose you are too this

evening. I hope you didn't have to work hard honey. What did you do there?

I sure was glad this evening when we had mail call. I got two letters, one from you honey and one from Mom. I got that lovely picture honey. If I ever was proud, I was when I saw it. I almost cried when I saw your lovely face again. You sure are lovely and the picture is so good too. I showed it to the fellows here and they said it was as nice a picture they ever saw. They said to me, "I bet you hated to leave that behind" and I said, "You're telling me." I showed it to my Corporal, he said, "You should be proud of that." He said I could keep it on the shelf beside my bed and I sure will, and I will take good care of it. Honey, I kissed you as soon as I saw the picture. Boy honey, it sure is lovely.

I sure wish I could see you at work. It sure would look fine to me to see you in your working clothes. I sure wish I was working there and we could go to work together. That would be nice, wouldn't it darling?

I kissed the letter I got today. I saw where you kissed it for me, so I kissed it good. So, we got to kiss each other, didn't we? Honey I always loved those kisses of yours.

Honey, I got my pass today. Now I can go to town. I can leave camp at Saturday at noon and don't have to be back until Sunday night. Honey I won't stay in town even overnight. I want to go in and have some pictures taken to send you as soon as I can for I know you are lonesome to see me in uniform.

Well darling, I hope you are not too tired tonight and I hope you like your job for I want you to have it nice while I'm away. Darling, well, I hope I hear from you tomorrow. I will write again tomorrow honey. I love you with all of my heart.

Your Loving Husband,
Merle, Love XX Love X

# Chapter 8

The town was Junction City, Kansas, the closest one to Fort Riley. Merle and about thirty other soldiers rode the army bus into town on a Saturday afternoon in late June. After the last six weeks of combat training, marching, and shooting, they were sure glad for the break. The last shuttle back to camp leaves Junction City at midnight. Merle was sure he would easily be on that bus. He did tell Irene he wouldn't stay in town overnight and he had no intentions doing so.

It was hot, dusty, windy, and starting to rain when they got off the bus, but the soldiers didn't care about the weather. Merle wanted to find a photographer and a Catholic Church. After getting that lovely picture of Irene, he wanted to send her one of himself in uniform. He also promised Irene he would go to church while he was away, and he hadn't made it yet. But first things first. Merle and his army friends went looking for a place to get a beer. It didn't take long until they walked through the door of the Junction City Saloon. Merle bought the first round using the forty-two dollars he had put back in case his furlough came through. He guardedly stuffed the change back in his money belt and took a long drink. The beer tasted good, not like the watered-down stuff he got at camp. At camp, he could only have two bottles at a time. Today, he would have his fill. The saloon was full of soldiers, male and female. Everyone was getting a little tipsy a little too fast. Merle downed his third beer and got up to go.

He started down the street and spotted a Catholic Church right away. Good, one down, and one to go he thought. The weather had worsened since he arrived in town. The wind was so strong he had to hold his hat on with his hand and the rain was coming down in pellets. Before he found a photographer, he ducked under a storefront canopy to catch his breath. An elderly woman came from inside and began rolling up the awning. She took little notice of him at first, but finally looked at him and said, "Hey soldier, you better head for cover. I've lived in these parts for over thirty years and I think there's a tornado coming."

"Thanks Mam," Merle said while looking up at the dark clouds circling overhead. Still holding his hat in place with his hand, Merle ran back up the street to the saloon, fighting the wind all the way. The door was locked. Merle pounded on the door screaming, "Let me in, let me in." Suddenly the door flew open and he fell inside, the door slamming shut behind him.

His buddies from camp were still there and grabbed him off the floor shouting, "Where in the hell did you go? There's a tornado coming."

"I know, I know," Merle shouted back.

The bartender was trying to keep everyone calm and set up the bar with a fresh round of drinks. Then the lights went out. A loud "Oooh" echoed through the darkened room. Candles were quickly lit. Some of the female soldiers were crying and holding on to their male counterparts out of fear and everyone was sobering up fast.

The wind was howling outside, and they could hear an eerie sound like that of a freight train. Then the large plate glass window looking onto the street shattered and the weather came inside. The bartender yelled over the roaring clamor, "Everyone to the cellar." The terrified patrons stumbled down the narrow stairway. They ducked and crouched on the dirt floor in the cellar. The ceiling was only five feet high and the undersized room smelled of mold and stale beer.

The bar crowd huddled together for what seemed like an hour and then it became still and quiet. Following the bartender's direction, they cautiously crept back up the stairs to find the entrance to the cellar blocked by debris. They were able to move enough of it to push the door open just wide enough to squeeze through. When Merle pressed through the small opening, he quickly realized the saloon was gone, completely gone.

The devastation was unbelievable. The soldiers immediately took charge and organized into search and rescue teams. They worked all through the dark, wet night. The first light of day revealed the destruction. The tornado ripped a half-mile path through Junction City killing fifty people and injuring two hundred. Splintered woodpiles replaced forty buildings that included the Catholic Church. Miraculously, Fort Riley escaped that kind of damage. The tornado's course turned as it approached the outskirts of the army compound.

As soon as he could, Merle wrote to Irene recounting the horrible events of the tornado and assured her he was okay. He despised Kansas more than ever and prayed for his furlough to come through.

The seven remaining weeks of combat training resumed with vigor. The twenty-mile hikes were the hardest for Merle. He developed blisters on the heels of his feet where his boots rubbed. He ended up in the hospital for treatment and while there decided to try to get a medical release, so he could go home. He felt desperate and was willing to try anything to get out of this miserable Army.

Over the next several months, Merle was in and out of the army hospital at Fort Riley five or six times for various injuries and illnesses, bronchitis, sore feet, and pleurisy, just to name a few. Each time, he recovered and was sent back out on maneuvers. He begged Irene to quit her job and come to Kansas, so they could be together, but she never came. Merle had a sinking feeling Margaret wouldn't let her come. He wished Irene would stand up to her mother for a change. He felt certain his furlough would be coming soon. If it didn't he was sure he would go mad.

Instead of getting his furlough notice, he got a notice the camp was going to be split up and the men sent to different areas of the country in October. Merle got word he was being sent to Camp Hale in Colorado. He would be even farther away from home and there was no furlough in his near future. Angry and depressed he wrote Irene with the news.

October 5, 1943
Fort Riley, KS

Dear Darling,

How are you today pet, I hope well honey? We are leaving here before Thursday of this week. Some of the unit is going to Oklahoma and some are going to Texas, but I am going to Camp Hale, Colorado and do I feel bad about it. I will be even farther away from home. They tell me it is mountain country and gets cold as hell there. I'm going to ask about my furlough as soon as I get there. We will be one hundred miles from Denver. I will send you my new address as soon as I get there darling.

Well darling, I hope you are well pet. I hope I see you soon pet. I can't wait until I get you in my arms again darling. Bye-bye. I love you and am terribly lonesome for you.

Merle
XXXXXXXX


Irene wanted nothing more than to quit her job and take the next train to Kansas or Colorado, or wherever Merle was stationed. She wanted to get away from it all, her mother, her job, and Harry Barron. She was praying Merle would get his furlough soon and maybe after he was home for a while she would feel differently. September was the month their baby would have been born and she couldn't stop thinking what it would be like to have her own child right now to love and care for.

It seemed everyone she knew was either expecting or already had children. Vince had two little girls now. Yes, she was bitter about losing her baby last March and while in that frame of mind, she wrote a scathing letter to Merle, now in Colorado, telling him how miserable and sad she was and blaming him for it.

October 15, 1943
Camp Hale
Pando, Colorado

Dear Darling Wife,
Well, darling I got a letter from you today. I was glad to hear from you pet but sorry to hear that you are still having trouble honey. My darling, I wish I could be home, so I could help you pet. I sure am missing you. I just think and worry about you all the time. I sure will be glad when November comes. I will get my furlough and get to see you again darling wife. My, this is terrible to live like this. When I get home to stay, we are going to settle down and live a happy life. I never will carry on like I did honey. I just can't wait until I get home to you and be a real good husband for you pet. I really appreciate one thing I got in the army and that is to find out how nice I had it at home with you. So darling the army did do one good thing for you for I sure realize I did not treat you right when I was home but honey I just knew all of this was coming and I was worrying and then I got so mean with you. But now darling when I get home to stay you will find me a different husband. Honey you know I was worrying about coming to the army and that's why I just did not care what happened and I drank so dam much

and just got crazy and treated you so mean. Honey I sure did wrong to be mean with you for I had no reason to be. You treated me so good and I realized it too late. But now pet I realize we can live happily when I get home for this army sure has changed my mind. Darling, I promise you I will be that old Merle you asked me to be.

I feel so sorry that we lost our baby and I realize now I was the one that caused it all. If I had done right and treated you right, we would have a child today honey. I just can't think I was so mean and hateful and caused all of those things to happen to you honey. Well honey if you forgive me for that this time I will never let myself be that way again. When I get home again honey, I really want a child and I know you always did pet. I know if we can have one of our own, it will be much nicer for us. We will have something more to live for then. I think of you all of the time and I am so lonesome for you honey. You are the joy of my life, and you are the only one I long for and live for these days. I hope and pray I soon will be home to stay. Love and kisses for you sweetheart.

Your Loving Husband,
Merle
XXXXXXXXX
And a million
more

# Chapter 9

Merle's long-awaited furlough began on November 10, 1943. He would be home over Thanksgiving but had to go back before Christmas. Irene picked him up at the bus station in Blakely where they had their last kiss, in the rain, six months ago. They went straight home to work on making that baby they both wanted so badly.

His homecoming was just what the two of them needed. Irene had saved up her vacation days at The Mill, so she didn't have to work while Merle was on leave. There were no fights and they were inseparable. Merle did go out to a few beer gardens with his old friends, who were still around, a couple of times, but he spent most of his time with Irene and her family, particularly with Frank. He enjoyed working on the Ford making sure it was ready for Irene to drive to work in the cold weather.

Two days after Thanksgiving, Irene and Merle were at home enjoying leftovers and relaxing when someone began pounding on the door. Merle opened the door to find Eddie on the verge of tears. "What's wrong Eddie?" Irene said touching him affectionately on the shoulder.

"Dad was in a car wreck on his way home from work." Eddie explained. "Vince and Mom are taking him to the hospital now. He hit his head on the steering wheel, there's a lot of blood."

Merle said," Are you okay, can you drive?" Eddie nodded. "Then we will follow you." They sped to the Blakely hospital and met Margaret and Vince in the waiting room. Merle immediately went to Margaret and said, "How's Frank, what happened?" No one knew exactly what happened, just that Mr. O'Donnell spotted his car over the bank near the homestead, and when he went to investigate, he saw Frank passed out behind the wheel. There was blood everywhere.

Irene scanned the room before asking, "Where's Grace and Shirley?"

Margaret said, "Mrs. O'Donnell offered to look after them. They can't see their dad like this."

Dr. Young soon entered the waiting area and went directly to Margaret, who was holding up very well. He said, "Frank has a concussion and a nasty gash in his head, but he will be all right. I sewed up the wound with twenty stitches and I want to keep him overnight for observation."

"Thank-you" she replied exhaling in relief. "Can we see him yet?" she asked.

"Yes, but only two at a time," he said. Margaret and Irene went in to see him first. He was sedated and groggy but awake. Margaret, trying to hold back tears, leaned over the bed railing and gave him a kiss on the cheek. Irene felt funny watching because she never saw her parents kiss before. It was just something they didn't do in front of the kids.

"I think there must have been an icy spot on the road. The car went out of control," Frank mumbled. Then he ordered, "Get my clothes; I'm ready to go home."

"Oh no you don't." Margaret ordered right back. "Dr. Young wants to keep you in the hospital overnight to keep an eye on that concussion." Merle and Eddie came in next to see him and convinced him it was best to stay overnight. Frank grudgingly agreed and the told them to leave. Whatever they gave him for pain was kicking in and he couldn't keep his eyes open any longer.

Frank left the hospital the next day suffering with a slight headache. He was to stay home from work for thirty days and rest until the cut on his head healed. Frank argued, "I can't miss work for a month, Christmas is just around the corner and I have to take care of the wells too."

"Suit yourself Frank, but I really recommend you take it easy." Dr. Young stated as he wrote on his chart.

Frank did stay home for a few days but at Margaret's urging, he reported to work at the Valvoline only four days after the accident. She was worried how they could get any Christmas gifts this year if he missed any more work.

Frank used the days off to get the Ford running again. He felt fine and the gash in his forehead looked good. He was glad to get back to work and reported to his job site at 7:00 a.m. sharp on December 4. He started to feel lightheaded and dizzy right before lunchtime and the next thing he could remember, he was lying in bed surrounded by his whole family. They were a blur to him and for a while, Frank thought he was dreaming. He could hear voices but couldn't tell who was talking.

Vince showed up at the homestead in a frenzy and pulled Irene, Merle, and Eddie out of the bedroom. "Now tell me what happened." Merle told the story. As far as they knew, Frank went to work that morning but never returned to work after his lunch break. His foreman discovered he just got in his car and drove away with no explanation at all. Frank Taft never acted this way and since he was just in a car accident, his foreman drove to the homestead to see if he went home. He was not at home. Eddie and Margaret went to Irene and Merle's house. The four of them began searching everywhere Frank might go. The checked the wells, his shed, and then checked his local watering holes. He was not at the Barrel, or the Dew Drop Inn. Next, they drove to the County Line and finally they spotted his Ford at the Point Bar in Shawville. Margaret was fuming by now, thinking he walked out of work just so he could get a drink, but when they rushed into the bar, they soon realized something was very wrong. Frank had a blank look on his face and didn't even recognize them. He didn't seem to realize where he was. They took him home and now they were waiting for Dr. Young.

Dr. Young insisted he have complete bed rest until after Christmas to allow his brain to heal from the head injury suffered during the car crash. Margaret felt guilty for pressuring him to go back to work when he wasn't ready to but still didn't know what they would do about Christmas. That night she pulled the gold rosary beads out of her bedside stand, snuggled up to Frank and prayed. "I believe in God the Father Almighty..." and she drifted off to much needed sleep.

Merle's furlough ended on December 10 and Irene took him to Blakely once again to catch the bus to Pittsburgh where he would take the train back to Colorado. He hated to leave especially since Frank's accident. Irene wanted to drive him the whole way to Pittsburgh, but the weather turned ugly and driving was treacherous. It was too dangerous for her to drive that far alone. They clung to each other once again, this time alone shivering in the icy, freezing rain. The bus pulled away and Irene smiled at the thought she could be pregnant. The possibility of it gave her hope and she tried to cheer up while navigating the icy road home.

# Chapter 10

Irene returned to work the day after Merle left only to find Harry Barron waiting for her as soon as she punched her time card. "Irene, how's your old man? How does he like the Army?" Irene walked past him without answering. He grabbed her by the arm and with a yank, swung her around, and pulled her down close to his face. "Answer me when I talk to you," he bellowed. Irene almost vomited at the smell of his breath and pulled herself away running to the safety of the crowd inside. She was so shaken; her heart was beating out of her chest. Who could she report him to? He couldn't treat her like that. However, there was no one to report him to. Women in The Mill had no rights and the men that still worked there resented them. There was no one that would listen to her complaints about her boss. Irene struggled to get through the day. That night she wrote to Merle.

December 15, 1943
R.D. 2
Shawville, PA

Dearest Merle,
Sweetheart, I feel so lonesome since you left. The only thing that makes me happy is the thought that we might be expecting a baby. We sure tried hard enough while you were home didn't we honey?

I had trouble driving home from Blakely after your bus pulled out. The roads were slushy and icy, but I made it home eventually.

I feel like I am catching a cold and I don't feel very well. I started to feel sick at work today. Harry Barron was his same old self on my first day back. I can't wait until I can quit that job and just stay home and take care of you.

Dad doesn't seem to be much better and Mom keeps nagging at him to go back to work so she can have some money for Christmas. I've been staying at their house to help when I can, but sometimes it seems like "Midnight in a Madhouse" over there. Grace and Shirley don't really realize how sick Dad is, and it is just as well.

Christmas is going to be so lonesome without you darling. I hope things get better around here so Shirley can have a good birthday party. She will be six years old this year. It seems like she was just
born yesterday.

I feel so bad that you have to be in that cold awful place over Christmas. It just doesn't seem right for us to have to live this way. I'm so sad.

Well, bye-bye for now. I love you darling and wish you were home. I want you.

Love
Irene XXXXXXX

Frank's condition worsened over the next few days even though Dr. Young made a house call every day. On the morning of December 23, the Taft family woke up to find Frank had died in his sleep. Dr. Young suggested he must have had a blood clot in his brain that was undetected, but no one knew for certain.

There was no time to contact Merle and tell him about Frank's death before the funeral. Merle and Frank had a special relationship born out of mutual respect and they had their share of fun together sneaking Frank's moonshine at the wells. Merle would be devastated.

The wake was at Irene and Merle's house. Frank's peaceful looking body, dressed in his Sunday suit, lay in their living room. Irene had to be strong for "the girls" and she didn't shed a tear as she watched over her dad through each night, remembering how he would circle her birthday on the calendar, wondering who would keep the wells running, and worrying about how her mom would ever get over the loss of her husband. After the third day, Irene picked up the guest register book and finally wept when she read the last entry. Scribbled by the hand of a nearly six-year old, the almost ineligible name read Shirley Taft.

Irene didn't care that she didn't get any presents for Christmas, not even one from Merle. She did feel terrible for Grace and Shirley. They had no presents and no father. Margaret locked herself in her bedroom for days, and for a while, they had no mother either. Shirley's sixth birthday came and went without acknowledgement. Irene prayed "the girls" wouldn't remember this awful holiday when they got older. When the funeral was over, she wrote to Merle and told him the sad news.

January 2, 1944
Camp Hale
Pando, Colorado

Dear Darling,
How are you today honey? I hope fine. I feel so sorry to hear that Frank has gone and left us all. I never was shocked so bad when I got the word. I sure would have liked to have come home but it is so far out here. I could have hardly made it home in time. I never thought when I left he was that bad although a person never knows what can happen. I feel so bad I won't see Frank when I come home again.
I suppose things seem funny around home now. I sure feel bad I cannot be home to help you. I am waiting for that day to come when I go home to stay. It really will be a happy day for us.
Well darling, I am missing you more and more but as you say, "We'll keep our chin up 'till the end of all of this for it surely will come soon." Take good care of yourself. I love you sweetheart.

Your Loving Husband
Merle
XXXXXXXXX

The United States and the Allies were making progress in the war effort in Europe with fierce battles taking place in Africa and Italy. Germany's Hitler had murdered hundreds of thousands of Jews and the Allies discovered mass graves. The surrender of seventy-six thousand Allied soldiers to the Japanese in the Philippines was one of the darkest moments of the war. More and more young men were drafted, including Eddie and Vince Taft.

Life for Margaret, Irene and "the girls" changed dramatically since Frank's death. Margaret, Grace, and Shirley moved in with Irene and Vince's young wife and two children moved into the homestead. Irene went to work every day at The Mill while Margaret organized prayer groups, reciting the rosary in a different home every night. Margaret and her daughters' lives revolved around war bonds, recycling, food and gasoline rations and prayer. Husbands, sons, and brothers were all fighting the war or dead.

# Chapter 11

Colorado winters were brutal, especially those in the Rocky Mountains and Camp Hale was located smack in the middle of them. It was common for the temperatures to drop to thirty or forty degrees below zero and snow could easily accumulate three or four feet in just a few days. Merle Heasley' most difficult training took place in this climate.

He soon learned he was a part of the 10th Light Division, a group training for warfare in mountainous wintry terrain. They utilized skis and mules to the scale the mountains.

The first thing Merle had to do was learn was how to ski. He was looking forward to it. It had to be better than combat training out in the elements of the mountain. His maiden downhill run was on a half-mile beginner slope. He easily glided down the hill clutching the towrope with all of his might. Merle picked up the sport quickly and soon moved on to the advanced skiers trail. Feeling overly confident, he went to the top of a steep, one-mile slope, pushed off with his poles and glided downward. The snow was blowing, and his visibility was poor. He thought he could see something ahead on the trail. After focusing as hard as he could, Merle realized it was another skier. "Get out of the way," he shouted to no avail. The next thing he knew, the two of them were tumbling down the mountain in a ball of snow, and skis and broken poles.

Once again, he landed in the army hospital, this time with a sprained ankle. While recovering from this most recent injury, he made friends with the patient in the bed next to him. His name was Clell and to Merle's delight, he was also from Western Pennsylvania. Clell was recovering from frostbite after enduring his first twenty-mile hike in the Colorado mountains. "The temperature was ten below zero for three nights and the wind chills got down to forty below," Clell told Merle. "Some of our troop decided to purposely freeze their feet so they could get a discharge out of this hell hole." He went on to say.

Merle thought about that way out and decided against it. "Did any of them get that discharge?" Merle asked.

"Only one that I know of, he had both feet amputated." Clell shuddered as he said it. "That's too high of a price to pay just to get out of "Camp Hell." Eventually Merle and Clell were released from the hospital and back in the regular army routine. The altitude tormented the two of them. The coal smog that hung over the valley caused a chronic cough. Merle and Clell both came down with it, nicknamed the Pando hack, named after the small town nearby that postmarked the mail.

They both wanted their wives to come out to Colorado and get jobs near the army base, so they could be together. "Evelyn won't even consider coming this far from home," Clell lamented to Merle one evening at the PX.

Merle took a gulp of his watered-down beer and remarked, "I know Irene wants to come out here to be with me, but her mother won't allow her. I keep telling her she's married to me now and she doesn't have to do everything her mother says. Boy do I miss her."

Clell emptied his bottle and said," Merle, we better go and finish packing for maneuvers. The next three weeks are going to be really tough."

"You're right" Merle replied and the two slowly walked back to the barracks.

Merle got off to a bad start the morning they were to embark on the three-week hike up the mountain. He hardly slept all night and when it was time to get up, he couldn't keep his eyes open. After drinking a pot of strong coffee in the mess hall and eating watery eggs for breakfast, his head cleared up. "Hey Clell," Merle shouted across the noisy room. Clell stood up peering over hundreds of soldiers, slurping down their eggs and he spotted Merle. He motioned for him to come over his way. Merle made his way through the room.

"Are you ready for this?" Clell said

"I'll never be ready for three weeks on that mountain." Merle responded. The two of them peered out the window at the ominous looking snow-covered mound looming in the distance.

The unit was to rendezvous at the base of the mountain at 7:00 a.m. As they departed camp, Merle and Clell mailed letters to their wives; the last letters they would write for twenty-one days.

The temperature was well below zero and the snow was about a foot deep. Merle strapped his forty-pound backpack on and was relieved it wasn't digging into his shoulders, not yet anyway. He swung the strap of his rifle over his right shoulder, tightened the hood of his coat around his already wind chapped face and was ready to go. Clell was in unit three at the head of the group and Merle was in unit seven. Merle was wishing they were together, but in the army, you never get what you wish for.

In front of the troops, a twenty-mule team led the way up the treacherous mountain. Strapped on their backs were food rations and supplies that the soldiers would need for the next three weeks. The mules provided a barrier to the elements as well as paving a path for the men who were trying not to stumble in the deep snow.

By the time they took their first break, Merle and many of the others weren't doing so well. As they ascended the mountain, the air got thinner making it hard to breath. The trail became steeper and more slippery. Merle felt as though his forty-pound backpack weighed one hundred pounds and his rifle strap was antagonizing his right shoulder blade. After eating mountain rations taken from the mules, things got worse. Some of the men got nauseous. Their vomit steamed off the white snow. Merle became sick too and felt he couldn't go on. However, on they went, up and up the precipitous slope. When they stopped to camp for the night, it was almost dark and snowing and the wind cut right through their clothing. The exhausted soldiers were ordered to dig their own foxholes to sleep in before they could get any much-needed rest. The ground was frozen, and it took Merle hours before he finished his and fell into it. He skipped the mountain rations this time and went immediately to sleep in spite of the cold, wind, and hunger.

Morning came too soon. The bugle was blowing, signaling it was time to get moving. Merle poked his head out of his sleeping gear and immediately ducked back inside. The temperature had dropped overnight, and it snowed another foot. He forced himself to crawl from the warmth of his bedroll and prepared for another day of tough training. Once again, the mules led the way. At once, they came upon pine trees growing straight up on the side of the mountain. The mule trodden trail, now covered with pine needles, made walking even more difficult. It became so steep and slippery, even the mules were losing their footing. They were tethered together with rope and when one went down, all twenty of them fell, tumbling into the trees and breaking the rope. Squealing whinnies was all the soldiers heard as the mules slid down the mountain directly into the troops obediently following behind them. The men scattered out of formation and the mules galloped off in all directions taking the rations and supplies with them. It was futile to try to retrieve them. Now with no food or supplies, the soldiers were ordered to return to base.

The three-week maneuver turned into a three-day maneuver to the relief of all. After three exhausting days, Merle climbed into his bunk at camp without even taking off his clothes and read the latest letter from Irene. Irene's news only made him more lonesome and depressed. She was not expecting a baby and she too was lonesome and depressed. He prayed that something good would enter into their lives, he felt they really needed a break.

## Chapter 12

Merle and Clell got a three-day pass and they couldn't decide what to do with it. Should they go to Denver or Leadville? They wanted to take the one-hour trip to Denver but neither of them had enough money for bus fare and lodging in Denver was expensive; too expensive for their meager budgets.

Leadville was only five miles from Camp Hale. They could drive there for the evening and drive back. The only drawback was, since army training began there, Leadville was off limits to the soldiers because of the massive number of prostitutes that set up operations there. Now, this rule was relaxed, and the inhabitants of Camp Hale could venture there if they dared. The soldiers could only speculate why.

"I have to get out of camp or I'll go crazy," Clell pleaded to Merle.

"Where do you want to go, Leadville, and try to get lucky?" Merle joked. Clell threw his empty beer bottle at him, missing his target intentionally and said, "No, I would never do that to Evelyn and you know it. Let's go just for fun, it will be a swell time."

"No, Irene would never forgive me if I went there. She knows all about Leadville. Her cousin was stationed here and told her about the whores that mess around down there."

"She doesn't have to know. How would she ever find out?" Clell begged. After a few more beers, Clell said, "Come on Merle, I can get my buddy's Jeep and we can be there in ten minutes."

"Okay, let's go before I change my mind. Maybe I can find a birthday present for Irene there." and Merle pulled on his coat and gloves. They jumped into the Jeep not feeling the cold even though the temperature was only ten degrees. Clell started the engine and off they went.

Before long, they were descending a steep grade. It was the north end of Harrison Avenue, the main street into Leadville. Heading south on Harrison, they looked down the wide, dirt road lined with parked cars and trucks. At the end of the street, they could see the rising slope of the base of the Rocky Mountains with a row of evergreens spiraling upward as if they were leading a path to the snow-covered peaks. The trees gradually disappeared into the white cap that topped off the gigantic mound.

At first glance, the town appeared innocent enough. The first structure they saw was a little Catholic church with a bell in the steeple. There was no sign of unsavory women roaming the streets, as rumor had it. Farther down the street, a large oval vacancy sign blinked annoyingly in yellow letters indicating there were rooms available at The Mountain View Hotel. There was also a bank, a five and dime store, a drug store and a jewelry store. Across the street from the hotel was a movie theater. The marquee read Tonight's Feature, *Mutiny on The Bounty*, Featuring Clark Gable. "I always hated Clark Gable, but women seem to love him." Clell remarked.

"I'm with you. I think he looks like a gangster. I don't know what the attraction is. I know Irene thinks he's great. How about Evelyn?"

"Oh yeh, ever since *Gone With The Wind* came out back in '39, she can't get enough of him."

"Irene can go see *Mutiny On The Bounty* by herself. I wouldn't pay one cent to see him." Then Merle thought to himself, Irene always goes to the movies by herself. He never seemed to have the time to go with her, but he quickly focused on the next establishment along the avenue. This sign read, The Golden Nugget Tavern. Clell pulled the jeep into the closest parking spot and said to Merle, "We're home now Merley boy."

Merle started to resist, "Now wait a minute Clell, let's stop by that little jewelry store first so I can get something for Reeny's birthday."

"We have all night to do that. Aren't you thirsty?"

"Actually, I'm parched. Let's get a beer first and we will check out the jewelry later."

They walked into the Golden Nugget, their mouths watering at the thought of a good tasting cold beer. The tavern was packed full. They could barely make their way to the bar. Once inside, they understood why there were no prostitutes roaming the streets. They were all inside the Nugget, working the crowd inside. Merle nudged Clell grinning and said, "These girls should be freezing. They don't have enough clothes on for a ninety-degree day." Squeezing in between two intoxicated women with painted faces and skimpy clothing, Merle ordered two beers and paid for them once again with his precious furlough money. Backing into a corner of the tavern with their beers, Merle and Clell watched the sleazy women take advantage of weary and sexually starved soldiers with expertise. It was a wild scene and the two soldiers from Pennsylvania downed their drinks, bought a couple of quarts, and left in a big hurry. They forgot all about getting Irene a gift and high tailed it out of town, glad of it.

"We don't need to tell our wives about this." Merle ordered.

"No way, my lips are sealed. Evelyn will never know about this little venture we had. Hand me a cigarette and open that jumbo." Clell said.

"Anything for the driver, you keep your eyes on the road. They lit cigarettes and drank carefully from the large quart bottles of beer wrapped in brown paper bags. They were on the outskirts of Leadville when Merle shouted, "Did you see something back there?"

"Back where? I didn't see anything."

Merle shouted, "Stop, stop. I saw something along the side of the road."

"Why should we stop, it might be some wild animal." Clell stopped despite his protests and backed up the jeep. They didn't go too far back until they came upon a dog limping along the side of the road.

Merle threw the butt of his cigarette out the window, opened the passenger side door of the jeep, and jumped out. He started to whistle saying, "Here boy, come on." The injured canine hunkered down and looked up at Merle with a pleading look of fear in its eyes. Merle gathered the forlorn dog in his arms and carried it back to the jeep, cradling it on his lap as he settled back into the passenger seat. Clell just shook his head and continued recklessly toward camp. Finally, Merle said, "Hey Clell, what do you think we should name him?"

"Name who?" Clell responded, thinking more about his last gulp of ale than their new passenger.

"Name the dog." Merle answered. Clell said nothing in return. "He kinda looks like Sarge, don't you think?

"Why do you think he looks like Sarge?"

"He has the same nose, don't you think." The two burst into laughter realizing the dog did look like Sergeant Belt. None of the soldiers at camp liked Belt and he did have a snout-like nose.

"Okay, we'll name him Sarge." They had to sneak Sarge into the barracks before they could examine him to determine the extent of his injuries. His left front leg was broken, and he had some bleeding cuts on his back. They put a makeshift split on his leg and cleaned him up. After thoroughly examining him, they determined Sarge was an English Elk Hound, not too heavy and not too tall. He had beige and brown coloring with splotches of black in his coat. Merle nursed the canine back to health and was given permission by Sergeant Belt to keep him on the barracks. Belt wouldn't admit it, but he was actually flattered the dog was named after him. Sarge became Merle's best friend, besides Clell, never leaving his side. The soldiers taught him tricks and before long he would sit, roll over, shake and stay upon command. It didn't take long for the army authorities to recognize how smart and obedient the dog was, so he was recruited. Sarge was trained in canine war tactics.

Merle and Clell planned to see Denver on their next three-day pass and they saved up their money to make the trip. Once again, Clell borrowed his buddy's Jeep and the two climbed into it calling for Sarge to get in too. Sarge took his regular spot in middle of the vehicle leaning heavily on Merle. Merle pushed him away saying, "Get off me you old mutt." Sarge just licked Merle on the cheek and leaned on him even harder.

The weather in Colorado took a turn for the worse in the previous weeks. There were three consecutive snowstorms in three weeks. The temperature would rise and fall creating a thaw and then a freeze. Even more snow fell, and the winds picked up. As they made their way down Highway 40, the howling wind produced a blizzard of blowing snow.

The wind gusts rocked the Jeep with a vengeance and practically blew it off the narrow mountain road. On the left side of the road was the mountain and on the right was a cliff. Clell was an excellent driver but even he was struggling to keep them on course. Just as they approached Shrine Pass, seemingly out of nowhere, a monster wall of snow came roaring down the mountain ravine burying them in a tomb of suffocating white powder. Sarge sprung immediately into action scratching at the roof and windows and barking frantically. Clell managed to roll down the driver's side window and began to dig desperately but the enveloping snow just fell inside the vehicle all around his face. Sarge kept digging and digging through the snow with his two front paws. He looked at Merle and barked as if to say, "Get over here and help me." Merle and Clell joined Sarge and the three dug with their hands, and feet with all their might. To their relief, a small hole appeared, and a piercing light shown through. Above them were people, people digging madly with shovels. The rescuers pulled them from their temporary icy grave and shouts of elation echoed through the canyon.

The avalanche was one of the worst on record in Colorado history. Merle and Clell didn't realize it at the time, but their vehicle along with two others were pushed off the highway down a three-hundred-foot cliff and were buried under fifteen feet of snow. Miraculously there were no major injuries and the search and rescue teams extracted the people that were buried alive and the dog too. There was a great danger of another avalanche occurring under the present conditions. The next day, Merle and Clell were assigned with other military personnel to fire heavy artillery in the snow banks to create a "snow fly" to prevent subsequent avalanches.

They eventually did make the trip to Denver, but it was an expensive venture. They went by bus this time and stayed overnight. Merle once again dipped into the money he was saving to pay his way home if his furlough ever came through.

Now he wouldn't be able to go home even if he wanted to. He needed ten more dollars.

# Chapter 13

February 15, 1944
Camp Hale
Pando, Colorado

Dear Darling Wife,

How is everything with you by now? I hope fine honey. I got the valentines from you and "the girls" today. I was sure glad to hear from you for I was feeling pretty low at the time.

I just can't get along much longer without seeing you pet. I just feel terrible living without you my darling. If I ever get out of the army, I am dam sure, they will never get me back again for it is not a life for a dog. I hate it so bad.

Well darling, I didn't get you a birthday present, it is so hard to get anything here. I know you will forgive me. Are your mother and "the girls" still with you honey? It is better for you to stay together, for it won't be so lonesome for you then.

Well honey, I will have to get you to send me ten dollars, since I spent it when I went on pass to Denver. I did not want to go out on a pass and spend any money, but I got so disgusted staying in camp honey.

Well, best of love and wishes for you. I hope to see you soon pet. Love and a good kiss until I get home.

Love,
Merle

Irene was used to sending him money and cigarettes and whatever else he asked for. With cigarettes at sixty cents a carton now, it's a good thing she was working. She was glad she never started smoking. It was just too expensive.

February 20, 1944 was Irene's twenty-third birthday. She spent the day working and the evening with her mom and "the girls" with little fanfare. She received homemade cards from Grace and Shirley and her mom baked a cake. Irene tried to celebrate and have a happy party, but she was still mourning the loss of her dad. His birthday would have been on February 26. After an evening of pretending to have fun, Irene wrote to Merle.

February 20, 1944
R.D. #2
Shawville, PA

Dearest Merle,

Well honey, how is your health? Mine is pretty fair. My biggest ailment is that I'm missing my darling so much. I wonder if you miss me too. I'll bet you do.

I sure was happy today when I got your letter. Yes darling, I forgive you for not getting me a birthday gift. Enclosed is the ten dollars you asked for.

My dad's birthday would have been on February 26. He would have been 52 years old. He always did enjoy his birthday so much. Do you remember how he would get a gallon of wine and we would all celebrate? Oh well, maybe he is better off than a lot of other people now.

Vince and Eddie haven't written for a long time. I hear from you more than we ever hear from them. Well, bye for now and I love you so very, very much. When you are home, I'll show you how much I love you. I love you to pieces.

Love,
Irene

It was a tough existence for the four female residents of Irene and Merle's rental home. Now that Frank Taft died, there was no man around to take care of those things men take care of, such as the car, the wells, the furnace, and shoveling snow, just to name a few. Margaret, Irene, Grace, Shirley, and all of the other women in the area did the best they could and prayed every day that the war would end soon. "Life is such a struggle to keep body and soul together," Margaret lamented to Irene on a particular difficult day.

Irene didn't really know what she meant by it but agreed with her saying, "I know Mom, I know."

The Head Well went down in the middle of the night and Vince's wife and children woke up in a freezing house with no heat. They temporarily moved in with Irene and her mother until they could decide what to do about it. Vince was supposed to get a furlough soon, but they didn't know exactly when and there was no one to fix the well. Then they were notified that Vince would not be coming home any time soon. He was deathly ill with pneumonia in an army hospital in North Carolina.

Grace and Shirley loved having their small nieces living with them, but it created additional stress and work for Irene and Margaret. At least now, Vince's wife and kids could get to church since they didn't have a car. All seven of them would pack into Merle's '37 Ford every Sunday and go to Mass. Then, just when they thought it couldn't get any worse, the Ford blew up. Ever since Roosevelt ordered the car plants in Detroit to start making army tanks instead of cars, there were few available. Irene was able to buy a used '38 Ford for three hundred and fifty dollars at the Ford Garage in Blakely. She felt fortunate because there were only two used cars on the lot and she got one of them.

It became so chaotic at home with all the kids around; Irene couldn't wait to go to work, just to get away from all of the confusion. She bid on a new job at The Mill mainly to get away from Harry Barron and to her relief she got it. Her new job was in the mailroom. Irene carried a heavy mailbag each day delivering mail throughout the plant. She liked it because she was pretty much on her own without having someone looking over her shoulder all the time. She also saw many different people throughout the day and she became friends with other women in The Mill. They were nicknamed "Rosie The Riveters" and they took pride in what they were doing to support the war. They would go shopping on their lunch breaks or go out for a beer after work always talking about their men who were off somewhere preparing to or fighting the war. These revolutionary women received a lot of press coverage and the *Blakely Eagle* featured a story about them with a picture on the front page. Merle's mother sent the picture to him at Camp Hale. He was so proud of his beautiful wife; he showed it off every chance he got.

The news reports of the war were positive and negative at the same time. The Allies were making progress. Despite all the good news reports, the casualties and death tolls rose every day.

Merrill's Marauders took back the Burma Road, a vital supply line for China. It had to be taken back from the Japanese and had to remain open no matter what the cost. The soldiers completed this almost impossible task, enduring inhuman conditions. The men succumbed to injury, disease, exhaustion, and the enemy.

The most dramatic news story was about the invasion of Normandy, later notoriously termed as D-Day. Hitler had built a twenty-four-thousand-mile wall called the "Atlantic Wall." It consisted of concrete bunkers, barbed wire, tank ditches, land mines, fixed guns, and underwater obstacles that could destroy the bottoms of landing craft. Forces from the United States, Britain, and Canada planned secretly to break down the "Wall." On the day of attack, the weather turned. There were heavy winds, a five-foot swell, and poor visibility. General Eisenhower had no choice but to postpone the attack. On June 6, 1944, the weather was still poor, but Eisenhower gave the orders to go. He knew many would not survive the day. The Allies' goal was to seize the five beaches named Omaha, Utah, Juno, Gold, and Sword. By the day's end, they did take the beaches at a great toll. Allied forces had over ten thousand casualties that day.

The horrific reports of thousands of Jews killed in gas chambers was the hardest to believe. Who could be so evil?

Irene thanked God every day that Merle just had to endure the rugged mountain training in Colorado and he wasn't in China or France.

# Chapter 14

By the end of June 1944, the 10th Light Division relocated to Camp Swift situated about thirty miles from Austin, the capital city of Texas. The climate there was a complete turnaround from the snowy cold weather in Colorado. It was hot, very hot. Some days the mercury reached one hundred and ten degrees. Merle thought it was odd his Company Commander gave them almost one-month advance notice of the move since they have always kept movement of soldiers a secret. Merle wrote to Irene, "I think they are trying to throw out the rumors going around that this is our last stop before going over." He didn't think they were rumors. Merle and Clell were convinced they would be fighting overseas in some mountainous country very soon. They once again implored their wives to come to Texas to be with them.

July 4, 1944
Camp Swift, TX

Dear Darling Wife,
How is my pet today? I hope fine honey. Well this is July 4 and another sad one for us honey.

The only good thing about this dam army is they allowed us to bring Sarge with us to Texas given that he is the best military canine they have. He keeps me company since I can't have you.

I have been all right, but it is sweltering hot here. I have sunburn on my shoulders and they are blistering. We were out one-night last week on maneuvers and the mosquitoes bit the hell out of me. They almost ate me up. We are going to have parachute training next week. If you hear of me getting my head busted, you will know I jumped out and it did not open. Ho! Ho! Well, they all say here that we will be in combat by December. I hope they are wrong, but I'm afraid they are right honey.

I was looking in the paper today. There are ads for girls for every kind of work and the wages run from $8.50 to $25.00 a week. Several places in Austin rent rooms to soldiers. Some are only $7.50 a week. I am going to Austin this weekend to see about a job for you. I know we can get along here darling with you working. Darling I am figuring strong on you coming down to see me before the last of next month honey, and I want you to stay a couple of weeks. Will you pet? I sure want you to so bad honey, so be sure and come darling. Please don't let anyone talk you out of coming pet.

Well I guess I will close for now and say I love you more and more each day and sure miss you pet. I am so lonesome for you darling. I hope I hear from you soon. Best of love for you darling and a good XXXX.

Lots of love,
Merle XXX

Irene boldly told her mother that she was going to Austin, whether she liked it or not. Margaret always had a strong hold on Irene and wasn't completely ready to let go, even though Irene and Merle have been married for over two years now. She also relied on Irene's help with "the girls" and her income. Margaret didn't like the idea of not having her around, but since Vince recovered from his bout with pneumonia and was home on furlough, she conceded. Vince got the wells running in tip-top shape and things were looking up for the Tafts. The time was right, and Irene jumped at the chance to take the trip to Texas.

Arrangements were made. Irene worked out a two-week notice at The Mill and paid the rent on their house for two months. Margaret, Grace, and Shirley could stay there while she was gone. Then there was the shopping. She didn't have anything to wear that was appropriate for the hot Texas weather and she had no luggage. She went on the biggest shopping spree of her life. She bought skirts and blouses, halters and shorts, and shoes and even new underwear. A sexy, black, silk, ankle length negligee with a low V-neck was a special indulgence she bought for herself and for Merle. Her favorite Texan outfit was a blue denim, knee length skirt that flared at the hem. To top it off she purchased a red checked gingham blouse.

With her bags in tow and a one-way train ticket to Austin in hand, Irene left her mother and "the girls" on the doorstep. Vince hollered from the driver's side on Irene's newly purchased '38 Ford, "Hurry up. You're gonna' miss the train." Irene gave one last wave and blew kisses to the trio looking out of the screen-door. Before they pulled out of the driveway, Irene checked to see if her older brother had a beer or a bottle under the seat. You could never be too sure about Vince; he liked his drink. The one-and-a-half-hour drive to Pittsburgh passed quickly and Irene felt happy and joyful for the first time in months.

They got to the train station in ample time. Irene was struggling to get her new luggage situated in the overhead storage bin when two good-looking soldiers came to her rescue and easily hoisted them above their heads and slammed the compartment door shut. The two settled into the seats on either side of her and struck up friendly, flirty conversation. "Thanks so much for helping me. I didn't realize my bags were so heavy. I guess I over packed." Irene said blushing. She rarely had the attention of two men at once and it made her feel pleasantly uncomfortable.

"It's our pleasure, helping a lovely young lady like you," the tall one said.

"Are you going all the way to St. Louis?" asked the blond one. "My name is Eddie and this stilt next to me is Joe." He gave Joe a playful slap on the head.

"What's your name?" Joe asked and quickly noticed the wedding rings on her left hand.

"I'm Irene Heasley and yes, I'm going as far as St. Louis and farther. I'm going to meet my husband in Austin. He's stationed at Camp Swift." Over the next twenty-four hours, Irene discovered the two soldiers were on furlough for thirty days. Eddie and Joe lived in St. Louis. Neither of them was married but Joe had a girlfriend he couldn't wait to get home to see. The two of them were part of the Fifth Army that swarmed the Italian beach near Anzio and after four months of savage fighting, took back Rome from the Germans.

"Just pray your husband doesn't have to go over." Eddie said to Irene swallowing hard to hold back the emotion that welled up inside of him. The recurring memories of death and carnage haunted him.

"I'm afraid all the prayers in the world won't prevent it. Merle insisted I come to stay in Texas before they get their orders to go across. They came to Texas from Colorado, where they trained in the mountains."

Joe looked seriously at her and said, "Did you say Colorado?"

"Yes, they are called the 10th Light Division, and have been training for mountain warfare in the Colorado Mountains."

"There have been rumors going around that there is a mountain trained division that is going to take a German occupied ridge in Italy." Eddie responded while flinching from the sharp nudge Joe gave him in his side.

"Where in Italy?" Irene asked becoming more and more interested.

"Oh, pay no attention to rumors." Joe said. "The army is full of them. The Allies are winning. You must believe that. It's the only hope the world has against that crazy Hitler." The three of them nodded in agreement, and then they nodded off to sleep.

Irene's traveling companions got off the train in St. Louis, The Gateway to the West, and her gateway to Texas. She was sorry to see them go and they both hugged her and kissed her on the cheek before they exited the train. "Good Luck. Take good care of that lucky husband of yours." Joe shouted from the platform outside of her window.

"Thanks, I will." Irene shouted over the loud whistle blowing from the engine. She waved goodbye to them and settled back in her seat, anxious for the train to get rolling again.

"All aboard." The captain shouted. The train quickly filled to capacity with old and new travelers. Her new traveling companions weren't nearly as friendly as the two St. Louis soldiers were. The elderly man and woman spoke not a word to her during the remainder of the journey. She didn't care; sometimes it took too much effort for her to converse with strangers. Instead of making idle conversation, Irene took the window seat and admired the scenery from the small opening, embedding every fantastic detail in her memory.

# Chapter 15

On August 4, 1944, the train that departed from Pittsburgh, Pennsylvania three days earlier pulled into the Austin, Texas station. The whistle blew three long consecutive blows to communicate in code their arrival. The passengers began to stir restlessly stretching their limbs seeking relief from the stiffness incurred during the lengthy excursion. There was no use trying to get off the train in a hurry. De-training the capacity maxed cars was no quick process. Impatient passengers jammed the aisles and recklessly yanked their luggage from the overhead compartments with no regard for the suitcases that were not their own, only to end up standing and waiting for the doors to open. Irene resolved to stay in her seat, peering out the window searching for Merle. The crowd outside her window was massive. There were hundreds of men in uniform as well as women and children. She saw no sign of Merle. The line of people in the aisle of the train began to move forward and Irene was finally able to stand up and stretch her own long limbs. This time she had no one to help her with her bags and removing them from the bin overhead was not easy.

She was able to touch up her lipstick before stepping off the train. The Austin train station was larger than she anticipated and hotter. The stifling heat hit her immediately, something she didn't expect, though she should have.

"Irene, Irene, over here," Merle shouted. She looked to her left and there he was jumping up and down wildly waving both arms high. The crowd grew thicker and gathered around her. Merle couldn't make his way to her and she was being shoved across the platform in the opposite direction. The more the crowd pushed her, the angrier she became. "Stop pushing me." She screamed at the top of her lungs, her nostrils flaring. Merle squeezed his tall thin body between people and luggage and finally reached her taking her in his arms and kissed her for a good long time.

He easily gathered her heavy bags and said, "Come on honey, let's get out of here." Irene clutched his arm so tight he was sure a bruise was forming. She didn't release her grip until they were far from the crowded train station and walking along the winding Colorado River toward their new living quarters. They stopped under one of the large trees growing along the bank and kissed again. "Irene, I'm so glad you are here. How did you get your mother to allow you to come?"

"I didn't. I just told her I was going, and she wasn't too happy with me, but I don't care. All I wanted to do is be with you darling." They held each other tight looking at the water flowing leisurely below them. Irene couldn't remember the last time she felt so at peace and happy.

The place they would temporarily call home was one bedroom in a house where they would share the bathroom, living room, and kitchen with other tenants. Merle would remain at camp during the week and would take the one-hour bus trip to Austin on the weekends. He had to return to camp by 7:00 a.m. on Monday mornings. Irene's plan was to look for a job that would schedule her weekends off. The first week of her stay, she helped their aged landlady, Mrs. Hubert, clean the house, and went job hunting. She explored the city on foot writing in her tablet a list of possible employers. Merle was right when he wrote there were all kinds of opportunities for work here. Irene's walking tour eventually took her upon the capital building. She gazed in awe at the beauty of the palatial structure. A wide tree-lined street led the way toward the majestic stone building perched in the middle of the city. It ascended at least twelve stories topped off by a dome high in the sky. Impeccably manicured sprawling grounds surrounded the structure. Pedestrians could walk through the ground floor where there were restaurants and shops. It was also a terrific short cut across the city block.

Irene's job search seemed too easy. She landed a job as a sales clerk in the children's department at S.H. Kress & Co., located on 808 Congress Avenue, not too far from the capital building. Kress' was an upscale department store that stood three stories high and carried every item you could imagine. She couldn't wait until Friday to tell Merle of her good fortune.

Merle's four best friends, Clell, Reuben, Mel, and Paul, were also successful in persuading their wives to make the visit to Austin. They all got together at The Garden on a Saturday night for dinner and a few drinks to get acquainted. The Garden was the local bar and restaurant where the soldiers frequented and were very welcomed there. To the on-looker, the five couples represented the typical military influx into Austin. Soldiers dressed in uniform with young wives dressed to the nines, hanging on their arms were the norm. Irene and Merle fit the mold. The mood was jovial as they sat down at a table for ten. Introductions flashed around the group and Irene tried hard to remember everyone's name. There was Lucille and Reuben Painter from Utah, Clell, and Evelyn Hughey from Pennsylvania, Francis, and Melvin Shoemaker from Maryland, and last but not least, Kitty, and Paul Penderson from Michigan. She repeated their names again and again in her head, hoping she would remember them.

The five young women bonded quickly and became friends, out of necessity, not that they particularly liked each other. They relied on each other five days a week for moral and mental support while their husbands were at camp. Every Saturday night all ten of them would go out on the town for food and fun. One night, Evelyn announced she was pregnant and had to skip the beers. Lucille was a little prudish and kept a close eye on Reuben's every move. Francis was trying hard to get pregnant and not shy about telling details no one really wanted to hear. Irene was trying too but would never reveal details like Francis did, it embarrassed her. Kitty was a tough cookie with a slang vocabulary and packed with energy. She smoked cigarette after cigarette. Irene fit somewhere in between these personalities and out of all of them she liked Kitty the best.

Kitty got a job in the Governor's Office as a clerk and she and Irene would walk to work together each morning cutting through the capital building on their way. They would stop and get donuts and coffee at a coffee shop on the ground floor and then return to the adjacent cafeteria and meet for lunch.

Money was tight. Irene only made twenty-five dollars a week at Kress', not nearly as much as she made at The Mill, but if she watched her pennies, they could get by. Each day she took only enough money for her donut and coffee and her lunch. After they ate their lunch, Kitty would lean back as far as she could on the hard-wooden chair and light up a cigarette inhaling deeply and exhaling loudly blowing smoke up into the air trying to make circles. "Hey Kid, do you want a cigarette?" Kitty would ask Irene every day.

"No Kitty, I don't smoke. I've told you that already. Anyway, I can't afford to smoke. How much is a pack now?"

"Paul got this pack for five cents at camp. Come on try one, what's the harm. I don't like to smoke alone. Just take one and pretend you're smoking just to humor me." So, after lunch, Irene would take a cigarette from Kitty's pack and hold the slender, unlit stick between her fingers occasionally putting the unfiltered tip to her mouth faking a puff. This satisfied Kitty.

Sometimes, the boys were not able to make the weekend trip to Austin because of Army training. Therefore, the displaced women had to endure two weeks without seeing their husbands. It was after one of these long absences that Irene, feeling blue, dragged herself to work hoping Merle would be able to come home tonight. It was Friday and she hadn't seen him for twelve days.

The children's department at Kress' was a delightful place to work when her supervisor wasn't around. Her boss' name was Miss McCarthy and she required Irene to address her that way. She was about forty years old and never married. "Old Maid McCarthy" is how Irene referred to her to Kitty.

Irene was waiting on a customer that morning when Miss McCarthy boldly brushed her aside while whispering in her ear," Watch me make this add-on sale" while picking up a patent leather purse from the display case. Irene stepped aside, her blood boiling by the rude treatment of her boss." Can I help you?"

"Yes" the customer responded and placed a pink ruffled dress on the counter. "I would like to purchase this dress for my little girl."

Miss McCarthy looked directly at the girl holding her mother's hand and said smiling, "Tell your mother that you want this purse to go with the dress." Irene was appalled at her boss' tactics and it appeared the woman across the counter was too.

The little girl's eyes opened wide and she said, "Mommy, I want it, I want it, please can I have it?"

"No, not today." Her mom responded looking now directly at the pushy sales-woman.

"Please, please." The girl squealed.

"Well alright." The woman quickly paid for the items, grabbed her daughter by the hand and exited the store, obviously displeased.

One of Miss McCarthy's cardinal rules was never open the cash drawer without making a transaction. Unfortunately, Irene accidentally pushed the open button on the register while organizing the sales slips. She looked around to see if anyone saw her to find Old Maid McCarthy glaring at her. "Irene, I told you to never do that. I'm going to have to fire you for breaking the rules." Irene threw down the slips and ran to the women's restroom. McCarthy followed her and found her sobbing in one of the bathroom stalls.

"Irene are you in here?" Miss McCarthy asked while looking under the stall doors for evidence of occupancy.

"Yes, I'm in here." Irene snarled back stomping out of the stall. "I'm three thousand miles away from home and I haven't seen my husband for almost two weeks and now you have the nerve to fire me. Well, you can't fire me because I quit." Irene fled the women's room on the verge of hysteria, grabbed her purse, and escaped the store leaving Miss McCarthy standing alone in the Children's Department with her mouth hanging open, now shorthanded.

It was almost noon, so Irene proceeded to the cafeteria to meet Kitty for lunch. She took a tray and began to order her regular vegetable soup and ham sandwich. "Reeny, are you leaving the Catholic church?" joked Kitty. "No fish for you on Fridays?"

Irene exchanged her ham sandwich for a fish sandwich and when she went to pay, she didn't have enough money. It put her over the edge after the dreadful morning she had, and she burst into tears. "Hey kid, calm down. I can loan you a quarter until tomorrow. What's up with you today?" Kitty led the way to their table for two with two wooden chairs. "Now settle down and tell me what in the world is wrong with you?"

Irene recounted her morning to Kitty telling her all the details of how she was belittled and just couldn't take it anymore between sniffles and nose blowing and a few bites of fish. "Here I am borrowing money for lunch and I don't even have a job."

"Don't let that old battle-axe get to you Toots." Kitty handed her a cigarette while lighting up her own. "Golly, jobs are a dime a dozen around here, you'll find something better." Irene put her cigarette in her mouth and defiantly said, "Kitty, give me a light." The two of them sat back and blew smoke into the air, Irene coughing like the amateur she was.

Their men did make it to Austin that weekend. The group had a marvelous picnic along the river on Saturday. They spread blankets along the bank and sprawled out on them. The women unloaded baskets of food and the men guarded the coolers of beer. "Hey Merle, give me a cigarette." Irene said taking him by surprise.

"Since when did you smoke?" He said looking at her in disbelief as he handed her his pack.

"Since yesterday, that's when." Irene said and then told him how she lost her job the day before and decided to smoke a cigarette to take the edge off.

"Don't worry Reeny," he said as he put his arms around her pulling her down on the blanket. "We'll manage somehow, we always have." What he didn't say was that the soldiers at Camp Swift got their orders that they would be going overseas within the month. They were told to get rid of their cars and personal belongings and to begin making arrangements to send their women back home. Clell and Merle convinced Reuben, Mel, and Paul to keep quiet about it until Sunday. They didn't want to ruin the entire weekend.

That night Merle and Irene made love quietly in their bedroom praying all the while that this time she would conceive. "I love you Merle. I want this moment to last forever."

He kissed her on the forehead and said, "If only that were possible. Listen Reeny, there is something I have to tell you. I promised the guys I would wait until tomorrow, but I just can't."

She pulled away from him and turned to look him in the eyes. "What is it?"

"The 10th Mountain Division is getting sent overseas within the month. We just found out last week."

"What's the 10th Mountain Division?"

"We are. They renamed us from the 10th Light Division to the 10th Mountain Division last week. I guess I forgot to tell you."

Irene was getting agitated now, nostrils flaring, said, "I guess you forgot to tell me a lot of things. When do you have to go over and where are you going?"

"We didn't want to ruin the weekend, but I couldn't stand you not knowing any longer. There is no set date, just within the month. They won't tell us where. It is top secret." Merle looked away from her, tears welling up in his eyes. They clung to each other falling asleep in each other's arms. Merle was dead to the world, but Irene couldn't sleep. She woke up every hour, sweating with worrying thoughts running through her head. Suddenly she felt like she was suffocating, she needed air and she needed to think.

Irene slipped out of the house unnoticed in the dark and headed for her favorite spot along the river. The park bench looking over the river was hard to find without the eerie light of her lantern. The bench leaned precariously forward toward the steep bank that led to the water. If she positioned herself just right she wouldn't tumble down the hill. After her feet were placed, she lit a cigarette. The stars and the full moon in the night sky gave off the only light. There was a thick haze laying on top of the water like a grey blanket that moved ever so slightly in the wind. She looked to her left at a silhouette of a bush looking ominous and swaying in the wind. A gentle breeze blew the woody smell of a dying campfire past her nose. The smell of a rotting fish lying on the shore penetrated her. The wind picked up and she threw her cigarette butt over the embankment and made her way back in the dark, silent, smoky night.

The next morning, she returned to the bench before Merle woke up. The images of the night were transformed. The thick grey haze that lingered over the water had lifted. The bush that looked so scary in the dark appeared unthreatening and sparse in the light. The odor of burning wood was faint. She sat on the park bench with a cup of coffee and another cigarette she took from Merle's pack. A flock of geese sat motionless on the water and a monarch butterfly fluttered past her face. The sun rose and with it came heat and humidity, unusual for early November, even in Texas.

This is where Merle found her deep in thought that Sunday morning. He walked up behind the bench and softly put his hands on her shoulders. She turned her head and kissed every finger on his blistered rugged hands. "I'm going to miss this place," she said. Then she abruptly ordered, "We better get ready for church."

"Yes, we need to pray." Merle replied not moving, not wanting this moment to end. After church, they all met at Lucille and Reuben's house for lunch. By now, the word had spread, and all five women knew their husbands would soon be in combat. The mood was depressing and distressing.

"As much as we don't want to talk about it, we have to. We have to make plans to get you girls back home." Reuben announced authoritatively. Preparations were made to get Lucille to Utah, Francis to Maryland, Kitty to Michigan and Irene and Evelyn to Pennsylvania. Lucille, Francis, and Kitty would travel home by train. Irene and Evelyn would drive Clell's car back to Pennsylvania.

Lucille, Francis, and Kitty were the first to go. It was a sorrowful farewell and they all promised to write and exchanged addresses, all except Kitty. She discretely left the day before without saying goodbye to anyone. Irene was baffled as to why her best friend departed without even saying goodbye. They were never told the exact date the

10th Mountain Division was pulling out, so Irene and Evelyn came up with their own departure date, November 25.

Irene sent a quick note to her mother, announcing her return home. The only postcard she had on hand was from Kress' Department Store depicting the decorated front windows with lines of cars parked in front. She thought now how stupid it was to be so upset over Old Maid McCarthy. What did it matter now?

November 23, 1944

Dear Mom,

Merle's unit is going over within the next few weeks. I'm riding back to Pennsylvania with another soldier's wife. We are ready to start home any day now.

Be seeing you,
Irene

It was a short message, but to the point. Irene knew Margaret was still fuming at the fact the she came to Texas at all.

Irene and Merle embraced and had their final kiss goodbye on the porch of Mrs. Hubert's house. Irene was determined to leave Merle with a positive and hopeful attitude. She would not cry. She would be strong, for him. She was until he was gone. Then she began to sob uncontrollably at the thoughts of her husband fighting the Germans across the ocean. Mrs. Hubert helped her inside and tried to console her with hugs and encouraging words, but nothing seemed to help. She was on the verge of a complete breakdown.

Just then, Merle walked back into the house. He had forgotten his soldier's pocket bible and he certainly didn't want to be without it. Not now. He immediately realized what condition Irene was in and wrapped her in his arms, he too sobbing uncontrollably. "Don't cry Reeny, don't cry." He said when he was able to control his own emotions.

"I'm sorry Merle. I was trying to be strong for you." She buried her face in his chest.

"It's okay. You don't have to be strong for me. I'm the one who should be strong for you. I just want to go over to wherever they are sending us, and get the job done and end this dam war. Then I can come back home to you for the rest of my life and we can raise a family." Merle said encouragingly. He gently lifted her chin with his hand and looked intensely into her wet brown eyes. "I promise you, this war will end soon, and I will return to you."

Irene began to feel better and blew her nose. "You know what they say; every cloud has a silver lining." Then she forced a smile and kissed him again, this time feeling stronger and confident that things would be all right. Merle turned and ran out the door through the pouring rain knowing he had to go, even though it was the last thing in the world he wanted to do.

The next morning Irene and Evelyn overloaded Clell's car with all of their belongings and began the long ride from Austin, Texas to Pennsylvania. Evelyn was feeling a little nauseous, being three months pregnant. She had a handful of soda crackers stuffed in the pocket of her dress just in case her morning sickness overwhelmed her. Irene volunteered to drive first until Evelyn felt better and climbed in the driver's side. It was a grueling trip, especially for two women traveling alone. After four days, they crossed the border between West Virginia and Pennsylvania. They were almost home.

Unknown to Evelyn and Irene, Merle and Clell were departing from Camp Swift, Texas on the same day, November 29, 1944, by train. Their destination was Camp Patrick Henry, Virginia, their port of embarkation.

# Chapter 16

The 10th Mountain Division arrived at Camp Patrick Henry on December 2. The division, consisted of four thousand soldiers and included 3 infantry regiments, the 85th, 86th, and the 87th. In addition to the men and their gear and artillery, the logistics of transporting the mules, canines, and skis was a tremendous undertaking.

"I don't know why this stupid Army is wasting their time on those worthless mules." Merle remarked as he reached down to pat Sarge on the head. "All they need is the canine unit with Sarge leading the way."

"You would think they would remember what happened on the mountain at Camp Hale when those donkeys fell down and took off running." Clell smirked. It was a humorous story now and each time he told it he couldn't help but chuckle.

Sergeant Belt strutted into the barracks prompting the two Pennsylvanians to erect themselves to attention, Sarge doing the same. "At ease, at ease." Belt quickly released them. "Heasley your dog is the last to be kenneled for departure. It's time. You will be reunited in Italy." That was the first inclination anyone gave as to where they were going. Merle tried to pull his thoughts together. He remembered Irene telling him something about a ridge in Italy, the soldiers on the train to Austin told her about. He wished he had considered her story now. At the time, he dismissed her account as just another army rumor.

"Yes Sir." Clell stepped in and began coaxing Sarge into his three-foot by four-foot box. Sarge looked sheepishly at Merle before moving.

"Go on Sarge, go on boy." Merle coaxed. The dog reluctantly crawled inside, and the cage door locked behind him. Sarge circled three times before finally realizing there was no comfortable spot. He sat down and poked his snout through the grate.

Due to the secrete nature of their mission, the Army issued an order stating no incoming or outgoing mail would be permitted while at Camp Patrick Henry. The soldiers were allowed to send flowers to their loved ones through the army conservatory before leaving the country. Merle's short note accompanying twelve red roses read: I love you Reeny. Your Husband, Merle.

Merle and Clell went to Mass one last time in the states both praying the war would end soon and they would return safely to their wives. Clell had a brainstorm while trying to pay attention to the priest's sermon. He took the church program he was holding and wrote a message to Evelyn in the margins, scribbled her address on the back and planned to ask the priest to mail it for him.

Merle caught on to what he was doing and followed suit. They approached the priest after the final blessing and asked him if he would mail the programs. He said yes. They could only hope he would. Of course, he would. He was a priest.

After two weeks of preparations and organizing at Camp Patrick Henry, the bizarre assembly of men, animals, and gear were ready to board the SS *Argentina*, a former luxury liner on the Caribbean run. It was a job in itself for each man to carry his overloaded pack, duffle bag, rifle, gas mask, and heavy steel helmet up the slanting plank to the deck. Merle found his bunk and dropped his equipment. The *Argentina* was clearly no longer a luxury liner. There was barely room to move between the tiers of beds that stood ten high. Merle and Clell preferred to sleep on deck, weather permitting, and they caught up on their sleep. They left port on December 10, 1944. The only bright side for Merle was his Army pay increased from fifty-four dollars to sixty-four dollars and eighty cents as soon as the ship set sail.

Once aboard, the men of the 10th were briefed on their mission. Even though Italy formally surrendered to the Allies back in 1943, German troops still occupied key positions in the Apennine Mountains guarding the route to the Po River. It was their job to take the high ground back, finally putting to the test the training they had in the Colorado Rocky Mountains.

Now that they were aware of their mission, there was nothing else to do but make the best of the time they had at sea. Merle would visit Sarge every day in the kennel and let him out of his box to stretch. There were movies on deck and boxing bouts on the promenade. On board were two

USO units that performed every night in the troop mess hall.

Merle Heasley spent most of his time playing poker and just walking the deck watching the waves when he wasn't in sickbay. The swirling waters of the Atlantic Ocean rocked the ship incessantly. He got seasick along with many of the other men.

It took the SS *Argentina* thirteen days to reach her destination, Naples, Italy. The first sight of land came after eleven days on the ocean. The soldiers crowded the decks as the ship sailed through the Straits of Gibraltar for a glimpse of "The Rock." Two days later, the *Argentina* sailed into Naples harbor, once known as the most beautiful harbor in the world.

The shores of Italy were a welcome sight to the soldiers until the brightness of the morning revealed their first signs of war. Rusty hulks of once great ships filled the harbor. They got off the ship and witnessed the war-ravished countryside. After being whisked through the bombed streets of Naples, they entered the town of Bagnoli. That night they were housed in a half-demolished orphanage where Merle was reunited with Sarge, as promised. After fortifying themselves with meager food rations, they hunkered down for the night sleeping on a cold marble floor. It was Christmas Eve.

# Chapter 17

Home never looked so good to Irene as Evelyn's father delivered her to her front door step. Crossing the old wooden bridge had no effect on her, in fact she welcomed the feel of bumping up, over and then down the other side. She was exhausted, emotionally and physically after the drive from Texas. She stayed one night at Evelyn's house. She didn't know how she would continue her journey two hours north to get to her home when Evelyn's father came to the rescue.

Margaret, Grace, and Shirley knew Irene was on her way home, but they didn't know exactly when she would arrive. Irene had no way of letting them know while traveling. Irene was grateful the weather wasn't too bad, just cold, no snow. "Won't you come in and have a cup of coffee?" Irene offered her driver.

"No, no thanks. I best be getting back home."

"Thanks again for the ride. I really appreciate it."

"You're welcome. Keep in touch. Come down to see my new grandchild as soon as he or she is born."

"I will. Have a safe trip home." Irene waved goodbye and walked in the house. "Hoo, Hoo. I'm back. Is anybody home?" It was obvious nobody was home; there was no car there. Irene was disappointed for she surely was looking forward to seeing Grace and Shirley. She suddenly missed them very much. She was anxious to give them the presents she brought them. She unpacked her bags removing the gifts and setting them on the bureau in the living room. The gifts weren't much, but it was the thought that counts, Irene told herself as she eyed the little cowgirl hats for "the girls" and a bottle of perfume for her mom, all purchased at Kress', the finest department store in Austin. As she was taking her suitcase to the bedroom, she heard voices.

"Don't squeeze the bag with the bread in it." Irene heard her mother's voice coming from the front yard. She ran to the door to see Margaret and "the girls" struggling with grocery bags. Unfortunately, for Shirley, she dropped the bag of bread to the ground when she saw Irene standing in the doorway.

"Reeeeeeeny" she squealed with delight and ran into her open arms. "You're home. We missed you."

"Reeny's home," Grace echoed, and she too ran to her outstretched arms. They hugged, kissed, and laughed. Irene looked up at Margaret and thought she caught a glimpse of a smile and a tear on her face.

"Hi mom. I'm sorry I didn't let you know when I was coming."

Margaret put her arm around her oldest daughter's shoulders and gave her a squeeze. She kissed her on the cheek. "It doesn't matter. All that matters is that you are back home. Let's get these groceries put away and see how much damage was done to the bread." Margaret said giving Shirley a discerning look.

The four busied themselves cooking dinner while Irene told her tales of Texas. She finally presented them with their presents. "The girls" wore their hats the rest of the day and Margaret immediately sampled her perfume, named "Yellow Rose of Texas." She was pleased with the flowery aroma.

After a few days, Irene knew she should be contacting The Mill to let them know she was ready to come back to work, but she didn't have the energy to put forth the effort and she wasn't dying to see Harry Barron again. Instead, she rested and wrote letters. She wrote to Merle every day hoping to hear back, knowing she wouldn't, at least for a while. Her letters to Lucille, Evelyn, Kitty, Francis, and Mrs. Hubert were answered, to her relief. She tried to gather information about the 10th Mountain Division's whereabouts from the scribbled messages. It seemed none of her correspondents had time to write letters, but did out of obligation, and when they did, it was in haste. Their handwriting made it evident.

Early one morning the florist from Blakely delivered one dozen red roses to Irene. The note attached said: I love you Reeny, Your Husband Merle. Irene, touched by the gesture, still had no inkling where he was or where he was going.

Upon closer inspection, she noticed New York City newspapers wrapped around the crimson bundle. She mentioned this to Kitty the next time she wrote. Kitty was quick to reply.

Negaunee, Mich.
December 8, 1944

Dearest Irene,
    I received your letter and was very glad to hear from you. I really felt bad when I didn't get to see you and Evelyn before I left Austin, but I felt so dam bad and blue about leaving. Irene you're not the only one that has felt blue. Isn't it awful after you've been with them?
    Have you heard from Merle? I haven't heard from Paul, but I didn't expect to yet. I sure wish we knew where they were.
    I got some sort of blanks last week on transportation from the government and I'm to get some check. From what I understand, it's for my fare from Austin to Negaunee. From those blanks, I found out that they must have been at Camp Patrick Henry, Virginia for some time because here's the way it was, my old station was…Camp Swift, Texas. My new station is…Camp Patrick Henry, Virginia. Maybe you got the same sort of blanks. From that, I thought that maybe they were shipped out from there, but then you had those flowers sent from Merle wrapped in New York newspapers. So, it really is a puzzle, isn't it?
    Oh, I forgot to tell you the good news. I'm expecting. I suspected I was while still in Austin but wasn't sure, so I didn't tell anyone except Paul. I have been feeling good and "Junior" isn't giving me any trouble. I hope your luck is as good as

ours is in this regard for I know how much you and Merle want children.

I haven't started to make any baby clothes yet as I've had the darnedest time getting flannel. Maybe I'll have to make them out of cheesecloth if they don't get flannel in the stores soon. Ha! Ha! That would be cute, hey.

Golly, I certainly do wish that I were still in Austin with Paul and having those good times together. Let's hope we can all get together again after this war. That really would be fun, wouldn't it?

Well, I guess I've scribbled enough so, I'll draw to a close hoping to hear from you again very soon. Keep your chin up kid.

Goodnight
Love, Kitty

After reading Kitty's letter, Irene was sure that Merle was in Camp Patrick Henry for a while at least. Maybe he left there for New York and that would explain the newspapers around her flowers. Irene tried not to but could not deny the resentment she felt after learning that Kitty was going to have a baby. First Evelyn and now Kitty and practically everyone else she knew. She tried to feel happy for Kitty and Paul, but deep inside she wanted it to be her and Merle, but it wasn't.

By mid-December, Irene had gotten used to not working. She looked forward to spending time with Grace and Shirley when they got home from school and helping Margaret around the house. Kitty was right about Camp Patrick Henry. Irene received a church program in the mail with a message from Merle scrawled in the border. The envelope was postmarked Virginia and an Army priest wrote the note stuffed inside. It wasn't much, but it gave her hope. The female family continued to cling to the words of the news announcer after dinner for the latest news about the war. The familiar tune that announced the news was coming up rang from the radio. WOSR, Blakely. The announcer began "Breaking News from London, England. Glenn Miller's plane went down in the English Channel, this morning. Glen Miller and his orchestra left London, for Paris, France this morning at ten o'clock, London time. The small craft lost contact with radio operators and it can only be assumed they crashed in the English Channel. As of now, no sign of the wreckage has been found." Irene looked at the radio, as if by doing so would clarify what she just heard. The announcer went on, "Miller and his band voluntarily joined the Aircorp and were overseas to entertain the troops. Some of their best-known swing tunes were "In the Mood," "Moonlight Serenade," "String of Pearls," and of course, "Pennsylvania 6-5,000." In tribute to the orchestra and the state, the radio announcer played "Pennsylvania 6-5,000" following the broadcast.

Irene was musing over the news report and whistling to the tune while absently washing the supper dishes. Out of nowhere, the vision of a sailor in white, bell bottom trousers flapping as he spun his partner came into her mind. It was the first time she thought about Ross Kepple in years. She was taken back and had to sit down, dishrag in hand and she wondered where he has been these past two years and what fate did the United States Navy hand him throughout this war. She tried to put him out of her mind. There were other things to think about. After all, Shirley's birthday was coming up and it was almost Christmas Eve. There was so much work to do.

# Chapter 18

Ross Kepple couldn't believe how quickly his world had changed. It seemed one day he was a happy kid with nothing more on is mind than the high school basketball championship and just a few years later, he was a man, a sailor, putting his life at risk every day to fight Japan in this crazy war. He tried to make the best of his situation but deep inside he was afraid.

After the declaration of war, the USS *Omaha*'s orders were to return to the Philadelphia Navy Yard and from there they sailed to and anchored in Gravesend Bay, located between Brooklyn and Staten Island, New York. Here the men had some rest and relaxation until each sailor got his next assignment. Ross got one liberty to leave the ship every four nights and he took advantage of every one of them. He gladly took the twenty-minute ferry ride from ship to shore and quickly learned the ins and outs of the largest city in the world. It was an exciting time for him and he took pride knowing his way around New York City, since he came from such a small town. He frequented Brooklyn regularly to see a movie and have a few beers afterward. It was at his favorite little beer joint he met Jeannie. Jeannie was short, much shorter than Reeny, and she had short red hair, so short and red, it looked like she had an orange bowl sitting on her head. She had freckles all over her face and laughed a lot. Jeannie giggled after every sentence, which irritated Ross slightly, but she made a huge fuss over him and he needed the female attention. Jeannie was a New York native and it pleased her to show Ross around the city. One of the movies he took Jeannie to was *Mutiny On The Bounty*. He really liked the movie but wasn't too nuts about Clark Gable even though Jeannie was. Ross and Jeannie had nothing in common but loneliness. She was no Reeny, but she would do for now. They became a couple. They saw each other every time Ross got shore leave.

Since Pearl Harbor, the U.S. Navy had the tremendous undertaking of rebuilding its fleet and regrouping to counterattack Japan. The war in the Pacific was raging and the Allies were losing. The United States and their Allies' plan was to conquer Europe and push Hitler and the Axis powers out of occupied countries first, thus the Pacific took a back seat for now.

Four months after the vicious attack on Pearl Harbor, revenge on Japan was initiated, Colonel William Doolittle had convinced Roosevelt that they could bomb Tokyo if they followed his plan exactly. In April 1942, Doolittle and his squadron took off from the Carrier USS *Hornet* in the Pacific and bombed Tokyo, Yokahama, Nagoya and Kobe. It was impossible for them to land on the deck of the carrier, so they planned to land deep inside China. Lack of fuel prevented a safe landing. Several of the squadron bailed out over rice paddies, two men were killed in a crash landing and the remaining were taken prisoner. Their mission was considered a success in spite of the casualties and it gave the United States their first taste of victory.

In June of 1942, America got a second taste of victory when they defeated the Japanese at Midway, a tiny island northwest of Pearl Harbor. They broke the Japanese code and took them by surprise with three carriers and two hundred and thirty-three planes. The United States wreaked havoc on the Japanese fleet from the air, turning the tides of the war.

Even though these victories gave the American people reason for hope, there were many more reasons to feel hopeless. Battles at Wake Island, Tarawa, Guam, and the Philippines were lost. After four months of fighting to take Guadalcanal, the largest of the Solomon Island chain, the Pacific fleet prevailed again, but the war raged on. Horror stories of the torture, hunger, and disease that afflicted our soldiers and sailors made their way back home.

Ross Kepple got his orders in June 1944. He was assigned to the USS *Alaska*, docked in the Philadelphia Navy Yard. He bid his farewell to a tearful Jeannie and left New York City by bus to Philadelphia.

The *Alaska* was the first of a class of large cruisers designed to be fast even though it had a very heavy main battery. She was commissioned at the Philadelphia Navy Yard on June 17, 1944. Early in August, their river run began. *Alaska* cruised down the Delaware River bound for Hampton Roads. She conducted intensive war preparation drills, first in the Chesapeake Bay and then in the Gulf of Paria, off the Trinidad coast. She then returned to Philadelphia where she underwent changes and alterations to maximize her firing power.

The crew of The *Alaska* was aware that the Japanese had taken hundreds of islands in the Pacific and were threatening Australia. To retake the islands, the Allies decided to use a leapfrog strategy against Japan. They would attack only the major islands bypassing those of lesser importance. In October, the United States began air raids over Okinawa, Japan and the Sixth Army invaded Leyte in the Philippines. There were unconfirmed reports of Japanese planes crashing into United States warships in the Leyte Gulf, the pilots committing suicide. The Japanese name for them was Kamikazes. Ross and his fellow sailors had a real good idea where The *Alaska* would be going.

In November, The *Alaska* departed for the Caribbean and after two weeks of routine maneuvers out of Guantanamo Bay, Cuba, sailed for the Pacific on December 2, 1944. They went through the Panama Canal on route to San Diego, California. They trained in shore bombardment and anti-aircraft firing before docking at Hunter's Point, near San Francisco. It was Christmas Eve.

# Chapter 19

Merle, Clell, and Reuben were assigned to the 86th regiment and Paul and Melvin were in the 87th. The quintet was split up; an occurrence they knew was bound to happen. Merle was grateful he was still in a regiment with two of his good friends.

Bagnoli, Italy was just a staging area for the 10th to regroup and the men of the 86th left there on December 26 by truck to Naples port. There they boarded an old Italian freighter named the *Sestriere*, which was so run down, it made the *Argentina* seem like the luxury liner she once was. After making the short trip up the west coast of Italy, they got off the freighter in Leghorn and loaded into trucks. The trucks took them to an advanced staging area near Pisa. As the trucks rumbled along the winding road, the soldiers could see the Tower of Pisa leaning on the horizon. They remained at this staging area for five days restocking their clothing and supplies. Extra blankets were at a premium once the soldiers realized how cold the Italian nights were.

The local Italians were grateful for their presence. They couldn't seem to do enough for the soldiers and even allowed their children to frequent their camps, usually begging for food or candy or whatever the soldiers would give them. One six-year old boy befriended Merle and would show up at chow time and eat with him. The boy's clothes were ragged, and he appeared to be cold and hungry. Merle would slice off a piece of Spam and hand it to him, then slice a piece and toss it to Sarge before taking a slice for himself. Once the three were full of the canned meat, Merle would let the boy wear his helmet and pistol belt around.

V-Mail was introduced to the 10th while stationed in Italy. It was a letter that folded into its own envelope. Once mailed, it was censored, photographed, and reduced in size onto reels of microfilm. The film reels were shipped back to the states and sent to receiving destinations where the miniature mail was printed out on lightweight photo paper and delivered to the recipient. The purpose of V-Mail was to ensure that thousands of tons of shipping space were reserved for war materials. Many soldiers found they did not have enough room in the limited writing space to write all they had to say. Merle used V-Mail to put in a request for things from home. There was just enough room to ask for cigarettes, handkerchiefs, cough drops, writing paper, and cookies. He still sent regular letters via airmail to Irene in addition to the v-mail. The censors would not permit any mail to detail military activities, therefore the standard phrase used to communicate they were in combat was "we've been busy," and through the month of January 1945, they were.

Merle and Clell would go to church services whenever they had them. The Catholic Mass just didn't seem the same spoken in Italian.

On the last day of 1944, the 86th regiment, moved out in truck convoy to Quercianella, just south of Leghorn, where they set up camp in tents. The rain poured down and the men trudged in the ankle-deep mud. They engaged in routine training and were ordered to pack most of their equipment into their duffle bags for storage. On January 6, 1945, the regiment received a warning order, in preparation to moving on to the front line.

The first casualties of Merle's regiment did not wait until they were on the front line. On the same day as the warning order was issued, a guard from the 86th walked off his assigned route along a railroad track and stepped on a German "S" mine. His fellow soldiers rushed to his aid detonating other mines in the area. This created a series of explosions resulting in the death of eight men, including the Catholic chaplain who so eloquently performed the mass in Italian. The men had no time to grieve. The next day, they entered the front lines north of Bagni di Lucca, relieving the 900th AA Battalion in the Mount Belvedere area. The Brazilian first Infantry was protecting the right flank. The left flank was essentially open with twenty-five miles of mountains between the 86th and the next Allied unit.

"Today is my wedding anniversary." Merle announced to Clell and Reuben on January 9. "I can't believe I've been married to Irene for three years and spent half of it in this dam Army."

"Congratulations," they chimed while rechecking their weapons.

Trying to cheer him up, Clell added, "We are going to beat the Germans and end this war. You will be back in Reeny's arms before you know it."

By January 20, the 85th, 86th, and 87th regiments were on the front line between the Serchio Valley and Mt. Belvedere. On January 21, the platoon, under the direction of first Lieutenant Donald Traynor, was ordered to send out a reconnaissance patrol deep into enemy territory. They had to cover twenty miles in horrible weather and treacherous terrain. To top it off, most of the patrol route was subject to direct enemy observation. Traynor chose four expert skiers to accompany him. The patrol consisted of first Lieutenant Donald Traynor, Sergeant Stephen Knowlton, Captain Harry Brandt, Privates Clell Hughey, and Merle Heasley. Yes, Clell and Merle had become expert skiers despite their initial mishaps on the mountains in Colorado. Their mission was twofold. They were to observe enemy movements and to determine the adequate approach routes to move their reinforced company.

Wearing camouflage whites, each man carried only a sleeping bag, skis, and his personal equipment. They went from San Marcello to the little town of Spignana by Jeep and at 4:30 p.m. on the afternoon of January 21, jumped off, and proceeded on foot. During the first mile, they gained one thousand feet in altitude. As they reached the top of the ridge, a storm blew up. They found shelter in a cabin occupied by British Artillerymen.

Traynor determined it would be best to travel at night and after a day's rest, the troop left the cabin under cover of darkness. They were able to move up the two thousand remaining feet to the top of the ridge, assaulting winds whipping around them. On the far side of the ridge, the patrol saw its first sign of enemy activity, fresh tracks in the snow. Cautiously they contoured along the side of the ridge, making their way with difficulty across the dangerous mountain. In snow, they used skis, but frequent rocky areas made it necessary for the troops to take them off and carry them. By daybreak, they had reached a point where they could easily see both our own lines and the German's.

Their mission was accomplished. They observed enemy installations near Mt. Spigolino and determined that a reinforced company could be moved through the territory, only if they were expert mountaineers and properly equipped.

By January 25, Merle, Reuben, and Clell were back with their company on the front lines when they were chosen for a combat reconnaissance patrol. It was a routine mission to determine if the Germans were still using an observation post located on Mt. La Serra. The observation post was located, and they found it fortified but empty. They stayed on Mt. La Serra for over an hour to make sure there was no enemy activity and then began to descend the summit. Suddenly, Merle heard talking and pointed to the others the direction of the voices. One hundred feet in front of the patrol was a dugout in the side of a hill. Smoke curled from a stovepipe at the top. The patrol withdrew and made plans for the attack. A four-man force would cover the open space in front of the pillbox while the remainder of the patrol was to cover the hill behind the pillbox. Merle and Clell were among the four. Reuben was with the soldiers covering the hill in the rear. The four men started forward to assault the position. When they had gone only six feet, two men came out of the pillbox. The two enemies did not see the attackers. Just as they started to move forward again, a third German came around the corner of the dugout. He was only twenty-five feet from the Americans and saw them right away. He let out a cry of alarm and Merle opened fire with his carbine on the first two Krauts while Clell put three bursts of submachine gun fire into the third. Reuben and the men in the rear of the hill also opened fire.

The German reaction was instantaneous. Intense pistol fire opened up and hand grenades began to land in the midst of the American fighters. One bullet went through Clell's hand, but he held tight to his gun grimacing in pain. The Krauts quickly maneuvered to surround their attackers. The squad was reluctant to withdraw, but it would have been suicide to continue. Mortar shells landed in their midst. Two of Merle's comrades withdrew first and covered the rest of the patrol while they retreated past them stumbling to the cover of an empty pillbox. The deep snow made it difficult for any of the men to move with any speed. Despite heavy mortar fire, followed soon after by artillery, they withdrew to safety, with no casualties and only one man wounded, Clell. He was taken off the front line and sent to an army hospital. By the end of the month, the troops of the 85th and 87th Regiments relieved the 86[th.] The 86th regiment moved to a training area behind the

lines to Lucca.    There they prepared for the
coming attack on the ridge.

# Chapter 20

It was difficult for Margaret, Irene, Grace, and Shirley to get through Christmas without Merle or Frank or Vince or Eddie around. There was no one to chop down the Christmas tree and set it up inside. Irene improvised with a branch she sawed off a pine tree herself, anchored it in a vase, and decorated it.

At this time last year, Irene just finished planning a funeral but this year she was planning a party. She was determined Shirley's seventh birthday would be one she would remember for the rest of her life. Grace helped with the guest list and Margaret baked the cake. Irene decorated and organized games to play, Pin the Tail on the Donkey, was by far the most popular. When Shirley's cousins, nieces, and schoolmates arrived, she was ecstatic. Irene knew she had accomplished her goal when at the end of the day, Shirley lay sleeping on the couch in her party dress, with frosting on her chin and a smile on her face.

Irene continued to write to Merle every day and by early January, began receiving his letters. Some of them were V-mail, and others were sent airmail. She was surely relieved to get those letters. When she didn't hear from him for several days, she nearly went nuts watching for the mailman. She did get regular mail from her scattered girlfriends from Austin. They kept each other informed the best they could.

January 9, 1945
California, PA

Dearest Irene,

I received your letter yesterday and was very glad to hear from you.

I am still fine and dandy as far as my condition is concerned. I sure miss Clell.

I got a V-Mail from Clell that he wrote to me Christmas Eve somewhere in Italy. I was sure surprised to hear he was in Italy but after thinking it over, I guess that is just as good a place to be as any other. Anywhere is better than the Pacific.

Irene, I have been sending my letters by regular mail to Clell. He told me he would get them just as quick that way. If he doesn't get them quick, when he does get them he will get a lot of news. Those darn V-Mails are worse than a postcard.

Clell is in good health. He said he had a long boat ride. I hope you have heard from Merle by now. This waiting for mail is sure awful.

The war news sure sounds promising today. I only hope and pray it does end soon. Keep your chin up and pray. After the mail starts coming regularly, we will both feel better.

Love, Luck<br>
& Happiness<br>
Evelyn

P.S. Junior is sure a lively character anymore. I'm tickled to pieces with every move.

Irene tried to keep herself occupied and made an effort to visit Merle's family at least once a week. Merle repeatedly told her that his mother didn't write to him very often and he was anxious for news about them. Frank and Sarah Heasley weren't the easiest people to spend time with. Irene tried to like them but deep inside she didn't. Sarah never liked the Tafts, especially Margaret. Sarah often said, "The Tafts think they are better than everyone else." She never treated Irene like a daughter-in-law and Frank barely acknowledged her presence. Nonetheless, Irene would go to their house and convey to them the latest news about Merle. Early in January, Frank became ill and was always in bed when Irene stopped by. Sarah revealed little about his condition. It only took seven days for his fever and nausea to wreak havoc on his body. He died on January 16, 1945. Dr. Young wrote on the death certificate, "Complications due to the flu."

They only way to break the news to Merle was by mail. Merle's mother refused to write the letter, so it was left to Irene to tell her husband, fighting the war in Italy, that his dad was dead. It was the most difficult letter she ever wrote, but she did it wiping the tears that dropped from her eyes before they hit the writing paper and smudged the ink. She had no idea how long it would take for Merle to receive her letter. How long would Frank Heasley be dead before his son even knew about it?

# Chapter 21

The USS *Alaska* docked at the US Naval base at Pearl Harbor on January 8, 1945. From a distance, the lovely island of Oahu that was shattered over three years ago looked like paradise with palm trees swaying in the wind. The closer they got reality became apparent. The crew of The *Alaska* quickly became aware of the lingering devastation in the harbor. Twisted wreckage of battleships, cruisers, destroyers, and planes were in plain sight. It was a somber sight for Ross and his fellow crewmembers knowing over two thousand lives were lost here, servicemen and civilians, and some of their bodies were still under the water. The ruined USS *Arizona*, now a tomb, where eleven hundred of its crew was lost, was the hardest for Ross to look at.

While in Hawaii, the crew of The *Alaska* underwent extensive battle training for two weeks and then they got their promised R & R. Ross tried to rest, relax, and enjoy these beautiful volcanic surroundings but he couldn't stop himself from buying a newspaper every morning and read about the allied advances taking place in Europe. A fierce battle was going on in a place between the border of Germany and Belgium called The Ardennes Forest. Each day hundreds of allied soldiers died even though the reports suggested we were making progress. This fight was in full force when the crew of The *Alaska* pulled out of Hawaii to do their part in ending the war.

On January 29, they left Pearl Harbor bound for Guam. Ross wrote in his journal that they left with 8 Tin Cans, 5 Carriers, and 1 Light Cruiser. The carriers were named *Sarah*, *Bella Wood*, *Bennington*, *Randolph*, and *Bunker Hill*. They got underway as a unit of Task Group 12.2 heading for the western Pacific. On February 6, they reached Ulithi, one of the McKenzie Islands. Here they joined Task Group 58, the fast carrier task force. At Ulithi, there were thirty carriers and various light and heavy cruisers. During the voyage, Ross speculated to his bunkmates about what lay ahead. He and never seen action before and needed some words of wisdom from someone who has been through this before.

The Captain sensed the uneasiness of his young crew and tried to reassure them of their mission. He spoke to the them over the public-address system. "We're on our first mission. We won't be close enough to shell the Emperor's Palace in Tokyo, but the carrier planes with us will bomb vital places near the palace and we will be backing the carriers up. We are a member of a large task force, which is going to pitch directly over the home plate of the enemy. It is our particular job to back up the pitchers. Let's all do a good job and we'll all get back and have a beer." Ross listened intently to every word and wrote them down verbatim once again in his journal.

After the announcement, Ross went back to work in the engine room and went through the thirty-six-step checklist for warming up the turbine engines on the ship. He had already gone over it so many times he could do it blindfolded but being the thorough kind of person that he was, he did it one more time, just to make sure. The pep talk from the captain didn't make him feel much better but he had to overcome his fears and do the job he trained to do.

While in Unit V of Task Force 58, The *Alaska* was assigned to carriers *Sarah* and *Enterprise* and the cruiser *Flint*. They carried out night air strikes against Tokyo's airfields. As they approached the Japanese homeland from the east of the Mariana Islands, the weather took a turn for the worse. The assistance of radio deception, submarines and long-range aircraft patrol were invaluable. Without these supports, they would never be able to accomplish their objectives. On February 15, they were one-hundred and twenty-five miles from mainland Japan. Once again, the captain spoke from the intercom. "In Task Force 58, which comprises VI units, we are unit V. We have 18 carriers, 8 new battleships, 18 cruisers, 80 cans, and 1 battle cruiser. Our unit is to do night attacking only while the other five units do daylight attacking." Following this announcement word spread quickly that a can got a Japanese picket boat and exploded a floating mine forty miles from The *Alaska* and a plane from *Randolph* got a Jap Betty Bomber forty-five miles away. *Randolph* also reported her unit destroyed one hundred and twenty-five Japanese planes on her first raid.

When they were seventy miles from the Japanese mainland and ninety miles from Tokyo, Tokyo radio went silent. The bombing had started. The raid continued into the following day. On February 17, the results of the raids were announced to the crew. The U.S. Navy clearly won this battle even though they lost forty-nine planes and forty pilots. The *Alaska* encountered light opposition due to the surprise element in the attack and the cloudy weather conditions. On February 18, they pulled out of the area to refuel in preparation for their next battle, Iwo Jima.

The Allies wanted Iwo Jima because it was strategically located seven hundred and sixty miles south of Tokyo. It was a vital link needed as an airbase for fighters' escorts and emergency landings. After patrolling the waters around Iwo Jima for nearly a month, the invasion finally took place early in the morning on February 19, 1945.

The USS *Alaska* was part of the Iwo Carrier Air Patrol located sixty miles out. Their carrier planes provided air support to the invasion. The US Marines waded ashore not realizing Japanese artillerymen were hiding all over the island in blockhouses and pillboxes. The first wave of Marines that came ashore were obliterated.

No enemy aircraft came near the carrier formation to which The *Alaska* was attached, however; other ships were not so fortunate. The *Pensacola* and *Ticonderoga* reported hits by Japanese shore patrols and it was reported *Sarah* was hit by three suicide planes, two on the hangar deck and one in the fire room.

Late in February, a new task force was formed. The *Alaska* joined task force 58.3, which had 18 cans, 8 cruisers, and 2 battleships, the *New Jersey* and *South Dakota*. It also had 3 carriers, the *Essex*, *Bunker Hill*, and *Cowpens*. Throughout February, they continued patrolling Iwo in support of the ground troops. One hundred thousand troops inched across the tiny island of Iwo Jima. The casualty reports trickled back to the crew of The *Alaska*. Ross heard there were over five thousand dead and over fifteen thousand wounded so far, and it wasn't over yet. The Battle of Iwo Jima was becoming the most brutal encounter yet of the Pacific campaign.

# Chapter 22

Merle and Reuben went to the Army hospital as soon as they could to see how Clell was. The bullet wound in his hand was healing and it looked like he would be rejoining them soon. They also briefly saw Paul and Mel when the 87th relieved them on the front. They were all very thankful they were still alive, even though so far, the fighting wasn't as bad as they expected it to be.

The men of the 86th Regiment rested and trained near Lucca. Mail and packages were finally delivered in bundles to each soldier. Merle joyfully grabbed his stack and went off alone flipping through the envelopes. There was one letter from his brother and all the rest were from Irene. He ripped open his package and grabbed a handful of broken cookies before reading Irene's letters first. The last one read:

January 19, 1945
R.D. #2
Shawville, PA

My Dearest Merle,
Hello my sweet heart. How are you today? I'm fine. This is Sunday and we are just sitting around listening to the radio.

I went to late Mass today. I prayed for you. Do you ever get to church? I sure was glad we went to that nice little church in Texas when we did darling. I want you to promise me you will go to services every chance you get. I know you'll go if you have a chance, if I ask you to, and I'm asking you to. So, that's all settled baby.

Vince's kids were visiting here yesterday. They sure are sweet. I sure wish I had a half dozen or so. It would keep me a little busy, wouldn't it sweet heart.

Sometimes I think I'm an awful wife to you. But surely someday, we will have better luck than we did before. We surely did have some tough breaks, didn't we Merle?

Darling is it cold where you are? I hope it isn't like Camp Hale for I know you sure did hate it there.

Merle, I hate to be the one to have to tell you this horrible news. Your dad came down with the flu a little while back, and three days ago, he passed away. He is buried in the family plot behind the log church. The fever was too much for him. I'm so sorry to break this kind of news to you in a letter, but there was no other way.

Your mother is taking it pretty good darling, but it was quite a shock to everyone. She is staying at your Aunt Gertrude's house now.

Harry Schultz is in Burma now and can't even write home. Fred Black's ship left for someplace called Iwo in the Pacific. Everyone says you are better off in Italy than in the Pacific. Let's hope they are right.

We really did have it nice in Texas, you and I darling. We sure got along good. My, but I'd be happy just to be with you, wherever you are, even in Italy. I'd give up everything and come if I only could honey, believe me. I would for I'm your wife and wherever you are that's where I belong. I realize that more now than I ever did before.

Well sweetie darling, I must say bye now. I love you more and more. Keep your chin up and pray and I'll do the same for you.

> Love, Luck and Lots of
> Kisses
> Your Own Wife
> Irene

Merle dropped the letter and sunk his head into his hands unable to believe what he just read. His dad was dead, and he couldn't even be there for his mother. It made him angry and he cursed the army and war. His brother's letter recounted the same tragic news. Merle cried himself to sleep that night as quietly as he could and took out his soldier's prayer book and just prayed.

Once again, there was little time for grieving. The plans for Operation "X" have been brewing for a while. This action would give the 86th Mountain Infantry, which are what they now preferred to be called, its first real test as a combat unit. It would make or break the outfit in the eyes of the other units and the enemy.

Field Order 9 came on February 15 followed by Regimental Field Order 3 on February 16, 1945. The mission of the regiment was ultimately to seize Mt. Belvedere in the Apennine Mountains from the Germans and open up a direct route to the Po River. The only way an attack on Belvedere would be successful was to capture the German positions on the adjacent ridge that included five peaks, Pizao di Campiano, Mt. Cappel Buso, Mt. Serrasiccia, Mt. Riva, and Mt. Mancinello. The American code name for the five-peaked crest was "Riva Ridge." The ridge provided the Germans a magnificent observation point. From it, they could see every action of the American and Brazilian forces. The Germans knew the importance of holding the ridge. Four times, it had been taken and four times strong German counterattacks had forced the Allies back. Now, the Germans considered the ridge impossible to scale and manned it with only one battalion of mountain troops.

Once the order reached the battalion commanders, there was plenty of activity. Men were stripped to the bare essentials of fighting equipment. Merle had to go through his duffel bag and remove everything he thought he would need. The bags were turned in and stored. The troops were ready to move.

Merle's company moved out during the night on February 17. They jumped off army trucks near Castelluccio and moved out immediately. By midnight, the long line of trudging soldiers had cleared Vidiciatico. Above their heads, piercing the pitch-black darkness were powerful searchlights scanning the slopes of "Riva Ridge." Between the men rolled the trucks and Jeeps, as supplies, ammunition, and equipment moved up. All identifying marks on the vehicles had been covered. All movement was made at night. The mules were abandoned early in the campaign, but Merle still had Sarge at his side. "I told you those jack asses were a stupid idea," Merle gloated to Clell and Reuben.

"I can't believe the Krauts on top of the hill don't know we are on the move." Reuben whispered to Merle.

"Thank God, they haven't seen us yet. It's just a matter of time until we come into the shadow of those spotlights." Merle lowered his voice and looked up at the roving streams of light above.

On February 18, the troops were given a last-minute recap of their mission. There were minor changes, but the ultimate goal remained the same. Seize and hold the ridge prior to daylight on February 19.

At 7:30 p.m. on February 18, the companies of the 86th Regiment moved out of their assembly areas and began the long tortuous climb up. The ridge rose fifteen hundred feet from the valley and from the bottom it appeared impossible to climb. Most of the trails were icy, and if they were not icy, they were either rocky or muddy. Slowly the platoons, struggling to carry the ammunition and grenades they would need, worked their way up the cliffs. Some of the soldiers had to scale the steep accent using ropes. After two hours of strenuous mountaineering, they had encountered no opposition. The men began to wonder whether there really were Germans up there.

It wasn't until the men were only four hundred yards from the top of the ridge they made contact with the enemy. A fierce firefight engaged.

- 181 -

The giant searchlights were extinguished. In the blackness, the companies moved in on the Germans, taking them by surprise. It took about an hour for firing to cease and the Germans withdrew. The troops dug in expecting the inevitable German counterattack. Now they waited for the sun to begin to rise.

Things were quiet until the following afternoon when once again artillery began to fall. The counterattack had begun. The enemy made their way back up onto the high ground and were able to isolate Merle's platoon. The Germans launched an unrelenting attack that lasted throughout the night. The Americans radioed for artillery support. Merle shouted to anyone within earshot, "If help doesn't arrive soon, there won't be anyone left to save." He got no response. Eventually, the American artillery began to fall but the Germans continued to attack. Once the Krauts began heaving hand grenades, the artillery observers ordered artillery directly on the position. It did the job. On the morning of February 21, after ten hours of fighting and with virtually all the ammunition exhausted, the platoon finally broke up and routed the attacking forces. It had repelled seven vicious counterthrusts. The 10th Mountain Division's casualties after the attack on "Riva Ridge" was one hundred and ninety-five dead and six hundred and fifty-five wounded. The five friends that bonded in Austin, Texas were not part of the statistics. The American troops had captured over one thousand German prisoners. They were now in a position to take Highway 65 and open the way to the Po Valley.

It was understandable that Merle forgot Irene's birthday that February in 1945. She turned twenty-four while he was in combat on the ridge. For the first time in days, Merle had a chance to write to her. The American Red Cross gave him some paper and he borrowed a pencil from Reuben. Knowing his letter would be censored, he wrote the best letter he could.

February 22, 1945

Dear Irene Darling,

I hope this finds you fine. I'm ok dear. I did not get a chance to write for a while, as I was pretty busy these days. I did not hear from you for a while, but I did not get a chance to get my mail. I expect to get it soon now.

How is the weather by now? I hope much better dear. I heard a radio playing last night. It sure did sound good, but it made me feel pretty lonesome to hear it. Do you listen to the news dear? Things are pretty good here now. I suppose you have heard.

I got a cold today. I don't feel too good honey. I hear lots of noise around here these days, but I have got pretty used to it by now.

I see Clell pretty often. He is well. Do you still hear from his wife yet honey? I wrote to Mrs. Hubert the other day. I hope she answers me. Did you get your car out of the garage yet?

I got my ration of beer again. It is six bottles every two weeks. It sure tasted good to me. I got candy and cigarettes too.

Do you see mother very often? I hope she is well. I cannot believe it honey that Dad is gone. I would miss him more if I were home, I know.

Did you look for a new job yet? I suppose you will be soon, when the weather gets nice again.

Well honey, I close for this time hoping I hear from you soon. Tell Margaret and "the girls" I said hello. I hope they are well. Dear, I think of you every day and miss you so much, but this cannot last forever dear. Best of wishes and all my love for you dear and a kiss.

Love
Your Husband Merle

As the month of February 1945 ended, it became evident to Merle the 10th was not through advancing, to his dismay. The plan was to drive north and capture Mt. Terminale, Iola, and Sassomolare, strategic German strongholds. Company changes were made, and Merle and Reuben were reassigned to 86th Regiment, Company G, now separated from Clell.

Merle pulled his pocket prayer book out and flipped through the pages searching for some answer to why. Why he was freezing in a foxhole in Italy fearing he would be killed at any moment instead of in the warmth of Reeny's arms back home? He begged God for an answer, but none ever came.

# Chapter 23

Margaret Taft was sick with worry about her boys. She kept her gold rosary beads in her dress pocket and prayed incessantly for their safety. Vince was drafted into the Navy and Eddie into the Army and she hadn't heard from either one of them for over two weeks. Irene was finally getting regular mail from Merle and he was in Italy. In Margaret's mind there was no excuse for it, since her sons were both still in the states. Each day that passed with no news from them made her harder to live with.

It was a cold February with a lot of snow and the war lingered on. Boys were leaving, some were coming home wounded, and others were reported dead or missing in action. It all depressed Irene terribly and she missed Merle more now than any time in her life. She tried to avoid her mother as much as possible. Irene spent most of her time with Grace and Shirley because they were young and fun, Margaret was neither. "The girls," never tired of hearing Irene telling the ghost story about the bridge just down the road. "Tell us a story before we go to bed." Grace said to Irene.

"Tell me a 'tory, tell me a 'tory, tell me a 'tory before I go to bed." Irene taunted her in a singsong voice while tickling her until they both fell onto the single bed laughing.

"Tell us that ghost story about the bridge." Shirley pleaded.

"That's too scary to tell little girls before they go to bed." Irene said knowing she was going to tell it anyhow.

Shirley jumped on the bed with Grace and Irene and begged, "Come on Reeny tell us."

"Well okay, but you have to promise you won't be too scared to sleep in your own beds tonight."

"We promise, we promise." They pledged together. The three crowded themselves on the small bed with Irene in the middle. Irene pulled the covers up around them and put her arms around each of their shoulders.

"It was a foggy, cold, and dark night." Irene began, speaking slowly in the lowest tone her vocal cords would allow. "Dr. Boone got the message to make a house call that night to old Sadie McDuffy's house. Everyone in the neighborhood knew Sadie was touched, a little crazy that is. She roamed around at night on the dark roads in her nightgown, her long grayish white hair blowing in the wind, and you could hear her screeching, like a wounded owl. This was a call the doctor made many times before and he usually found Sadie along the road, coaxed her into his buggy, and took her home where her daughter would thank him, again. This night as he hitched up his horse to the buggy he looked into the foggy sky and an unexplainable eerie feeling overtook him. Dr. Boone didn't want to go. He reluctantly tossed his black medicine bag inside and set out. Things didn't go well from the start. The fog was so thick he could barely see where the horse was leading him. He was grateful when he came upon the wooden bridge that cleared the railroad tracks below. He knew he was on the right track. His horse hesitated before stepping onto the creaking wooden boards, but with the doctor's persuasion, proceeded up the incline. As they neared the crest of the bridge, a cold wind blew up causing Dr. Boone to fasten the top button of his coat snug around his neck. Suddenly his horse reared up, front hooves high in the air. The horse's whinny pierced the silent gloom." Irene shouted, "Boom!" as loud as she would dare.

"Aahh," both girls cried out.

Irene held on to them tight and continued. "All of a sudden the buggy became so heavy the horse could not budge an inch. It came to a complete stop and then there was a loud crash. Dr. Boone fearfully glanced to his right and saw the bloody head of old Sadie McDuffy sitting on his passenger seat looking up at him smiling. He whipped his horse as hard as he could, and they descended the other side of the bridge going so fast they almost tipped over. As the wild buggy cleared the last board of the bridge, the head rolled off the seat, down the bank and disappeared under the bridge and old Sadie McDuffy was never heard from again."

"What happened to the doctor?" Grace asked.

"He was found slumped over in his buggy with his hand on his bag, a few miles away, dead. They never found his horse."

"Is that a true story?" Shirley asked clutching Irene's arm with all of her might.

"Yes." Irene tried to sound convincing.

Sensible Grace hopped off the bed looking at the two of them with her hands placed firmly on her hips and said, "No it isn't."

"You don't have to believe it if you don't want to, but I do." Reeny said. "Some of the neighbors claim they can hear Sadie wailing under the bridge, especially on dark, cold, foggy nights."

Shirley believed the story and Grace, even though her words denied it, sort of believed it. They never went near the bridge at night.

Irene tucked "the girls" in for the night and went to her own room to reply to the letters she got that week. Mrs. Hubert and Kitty were on the top of her list and then she would write her daily letter to Merle.

Shawville, PA
February 27, 1945

Dearest Merle,

Just sitting here tonight listening to the radio and as always thinking of my darling away over the sea. I was thinking of us in Texas and how happy we were. I was thinking of that last morning you left me at Mrs. Hubert's house, how I wasn't going to cry and then after you left I cut loose bawling. Then you forgot something, came back, and caught me crying, honey. They were all swell people we met there. I bet you think I'm silly writing like this to you dear, but I just want to talk to you and this is the only way I can for now sweet. We will really have time to talk about all our good times one of these days, I feel sure.

They made a new law here now that all the beer parlors and all places of amusement must close at twelve o'clock every night. I guess that's late enough to be out at night.

I sure wish you could be home with me sweetie pie, then I'd be really happy just to keep house for you and me together baby. Don't worry about me sweet. Remember, I always believe every cloud has a silver lining and it will for us too honey.

I love you darling boy more and more.

XXXXXYour OwnXXXXXXX
XXXXIreneXXXXXXXX

She put down her pen and looked up to see Shirley peeking into her room through the cracked door opening carrying her blanket.

"Can I sleep with you tonight Reeny? I'm scared. I keep dreaming of that old Sadie."

"Come on in honey." Irene pulled back the covers for Shirley to climb in and the two said a little prayer for Merle, Vince, and Eddie. They fell asleep in each other's arms.

# Chapter 24

Ross Kepple was praying too. He watched petrified as a Japanese Kamikaze plane crashed into the USS *Bismark* only twenty miles from The *Alaska*. The *Bismark* was blown into toothpick size pieces, totally destroyed. The search teams recovered only thirty-three survivors in the carnage. So far, this was the closest the sailors on board The *Alaska* came to death in the Pacific. They were still supporting the ground troops on Iwo Jima. Smoke and fire could be seen on the horizon. Then the firebombing of Tokyo began. The Allies were giving them all they had in an attempt to force Japan to surrender. The radio waves reported Japan claimed little damage was done.

The *Alaska,* still with Task Group 58.4 formed around the fleet carriers *Yorktown*, *Intrepid*, *Independence* and *Langley*. Her principle mission was as it had been before, the defense of the task group against enemy air or surface attacks. On March 12, 1945 she arrived at Ulithi and on March 14, they left there for the Ryukyu Islands, located directly south of Japan.

The battle plan for The *Alaska* was outlined in detail. Task Force 58 cruised northwesterly from the Caroline Islands and refueled at sea. The carriers attacked the Japanese homeland again striking their airfields. Planes from Ross's task force joined those from three other task groups sweeping over airfields at Usa, Oita, and Saeki, claiming one hundred and seven enemy aircraft destroyed on the ground and seventy-seven engaged over the target area.

On March 18, the Japanese retaliated with air strikes of their own. Task Force 58's radars provided no warning of the approach of enemy planes, due to the cloudy weather conditions. The first indication of the Kamikaze flying overhead was a visual sighting at 0800 that Sunday morning. The Japanese suicide bomber's first attempt to demolish The *Alaska* failed. The Rising Sun emblem was plainly seen by the crew that was stationed topside as the plane turned for another pass. Another Japanese plane came in and it too missed them with two bombs. The *Alaska* commenced fire and registered hits immediately, but the suicide bomber maintained its course and aimed for another target, The *Intrepid*. Less than a half-mile from The *Intrepid*, it exploded into fragments with a direct hit from Alaska's guns. At 0822, a single engine plane approached them in a threatening fashion from ahead in a shallow dive. *Alaska* opened fired and scored hits. Simultaneously they received word that the plane was a friendly F6F Hellcat.

Fortunately, the pilot was uninjured and ditched the crippled plane. Another ship picked him up.

The crew ate their lunch in three shifts that day, the first commencing at 1200. For the balance of the day, the suicide attacks continued. The combat air patrol downed a dozen planes while the ships gunfire accounted for almost two dozen more. The *Alaska* destroyed a second enemy bomber at 1315. Only thirty-eight miles from mainland Japan, The *Alaska*'s carrier units bombed Kyushu, the large southern island of the Japanese mainland including Nagasaki, Hiroshima, and the islands in the string of the Ryukyu Islands. From there they flew northeast and attacked the Japanese fleet in the Sea of Japan. The American fleet claimed March 18, 1945 as another victory after shooting down two hundred enemy aircraft and destroying two hundred and seventy-five planes on Japanese soil. They also sunk six freighters. Damages to the United States Navy included 2 battleships, 3 carriers, 2 light cruisers, 4 cans, and 1 submarine.

A shaken Ross Kepple was finally relieved from his engine room duty late that Sunday night. He made his way to his bunk and fell into it completely exhausted. He lay there trying to sleep but was unable to drift off. The battles of the day kept racing through his head. He knew morning would come with more of the same and he was scared to death.

He prayed he would be able to face whatever came his way tonight and tomorrow. Life beyond tomorrow was unimaginable.

He was rousted from his sleep at 0500 the following morning. Two Japanese planes were reported overhead. All hands-on deck. Ross got to his station just in time to hear that the topside crew saw a flash followed by a slowly rising column of smoke. At 0708, reports were that a carrier had been hit, but there was no confirmation on which one. Soon the radio brought verification that The *Franklin* had been hit by a one-thousand-pound bomb on the bridge. They had heavy fires under control within forty-five minutes and the engine room fire was knocked out. Top priority was to take the planes off *The Franklin*. Once again, the cloud cover rendered radar useless and the Task Forces were attacked all afternoon by Japanese planes. Eventually Task Force 58 was able to recover the crippled *Franklin* at the same time launching fighter sweeps against Kyushu in order to disorganize further air strikes.

A salvage unit was quickly formed to further protect *Franklin,* which *Alaska* was part of along with *Guam, Pittsburgh,* and *Santa Fe.* They screened the damaged *Franklin* and determined to speed toward Guam as fast as was possible. On March 20, the salvage unit escorted *Franklin* out of the area with The *Santa Fe* towing *Franklin* at five knots. By the afternoon, The *Franklin* got underway herself, and was able to sail at eighteen knots. At 1150, Japanese aircraft reappeared. Several unidentified aircraft showed up on the radar screens. Most of them were Navy PB4Y patrol bombers failing to show identification, friend or foe. Unfortunately, because of the friendly character of one, the interception of another at about the same time failed to materialize. Thankfully, the poor marksmanship on the part of the Japanese pilot saved *Franklin* from another bomb hit. As it sped away, *Alaska*'s big 40-millimeter mount fired incessantly causing flash burns on the men manning the big guns. Radar gave the other carriers his position and they got him. It seemed to be a miracle that they were able to save The *Franklin*. Once the situation was secured, fifteen of the wounded from *Franklin* came aboard The *Alaska*. Sickbay looked like a hospital ship. Men crying out in pain with broken legs, shrapnel wounds and flash burns filled every inch of space.

On March 22, *Alaska*'s part in the escort of *Franklin* was complete and she rejoined Task Force 58.4 fueling from tanker *Chiope*. On her way back to the Ryukyu Islands, they exploded a floating mine, rocking the gigantic ship like a toy boat.

Okinawa was the largest island of the Ryukyu chain and *Alaska* and *Guam* were standing by for the bombardment by the battleships. On March 26, bombers with eight rockets and five hundred-pound bombs left the carriers all day, hitting strategic areas of the island. The *Alaska* was detached on March 27, to carry out a shore bombardment against Minami Daito Shima; a tiny island with three airfields on it was shelled. It was one hundred and sixty miles southeast of Okinawa. *Alaska*'s Task Unit was ordered to carry out the shoot 'en route to a fueling area. *Alaska*'s main battery hurled forty-five high capacity rounds toward the shore while her five-inch battery added three hundred and fifty-two rounds of anti-aircraft ammunition. The crew of The *Alaska* watched as fires lit up the island. No answering fire came from the beach.

Rejoining Task Force 58.4 at the fueling rendezvous, *Alaska* transferred the wounded men she took on board from The *Franklin* to The

*Tomahawk* while she took on fuel from the fleet oilier. She then resumed looking for the Japanese fleet around the northern end of The Ryukyus.

Air strikes against Okinawa continued, setting the date for the landing to commence on April 1, 1945, Easter Sunday.

March 1945 was the most horrible month of Ross Kepple's twenty-four-year existence. He suddenly felt like a child and just wanted to go home.

# Chapter 25

On March 1, 1945, the specific objectives were laid out to the 86th Mountain Infantry Regiment. Merle and Reuben listened intently to what their role would be now part of G Company. Each objective was designated by a code name and each company was assigned one or more of the objectives. Their first was Objective Baker, the capture of Mt. Terminale and Iola. As soon as this ground was secured, they were to attack Objective Dog: Hill 921. From Hill 921 they would move on to Hills 916 and 879, the two peaks on either side of Il Monte, which was named Objective Fox.

Sitting nervously in their foxhole, with Sarge obediently silent and alert, Reuben cleaned his rifle again and double-checked his ammunition. "I know I don't have enough ammo. Do you?" He asked Merle.

"Probably not, but there is nothing we can do about it. There is no more. The captain demanded more but was denied." Merle said. Artillery fire from the German 170-mm guns began falling around them. They sunk deeper into the dugout waiting out the attack. The Germans have been shelling the area sporadically over the last two days and the huge shells dropped from the sky without warning. Waiting for the order to commence the next stage of attacks was killing Merle. "I would rather get on with this thing. I can't stand just sitting here." He moaned. Merle got his wish. On the afternoon of March 2, the uncertainty was over. The order came down that the operation would take place the next day, in accordance with previous plans. In preparation for the movement, a G Company patrol moved into the vicinity of C. Romito. The mission required canines to lead them through minefields believed to be in the path of a house that was an enemy stronghold. It was crucial to the entire operation for the occupants to be taken out before the morning of March 3. Merle and Sarge were part of the patrol. Sarge led them deftly through the darkness avoiding the deadly mines, but their approach was discovered, and they were met with machine gun and mortar fire. The patrol laid down a base fire while Merle and Sarge circled the house and approached it from the rear engaging the enemy. The Germans fled through the front of the house but not without a fight. Having cleared the house, G Company withdrew. The Germans suffered several casualties, but none to Merle's squad. They completed their mission and retreated to their foxholes waiting for dawn.

There was little sleep that night and by the early morning of March 3, 1945, Reuben and Merle crouched together once again in the safety of the foxhole gripping their weapons, waiting. At 0630, all was quiet. At 0640, the artillery barrage began. The 86th fired every caliber available, heavy, and light into the front lines. It went on for twenty long minutes. At 0700, before the last shells had landed, Merle, Reuben, Sarge and the rest of G Company were out of their holes and advancing across the field. The Germans countered with artillery, mortar, and machine gun fire. Reuben shouted over the deafening gunfire, "Merle, just keep moving. If we get pinned down, we are dead." Merle could not hear a word he said but looked his way and nodded in agreement. Sarge ran ahead of the soldiers leading them through a hail of fire, dodging every bullet. The company followed his direction and moved up.

Despite Reuben's warning, their platoon was pinned down by heavy machine gun fire. The disorganized group split up and Merle and Reuben found themselves alone with ten other men and no one in command. They moved rapidly across the slope and encountered two snipers. Reuben personally took care of one of them, but the other one shot wildly into the platoon. Before he could take cover, Reuben saw Merle falling face down. Then he saw Sarge running out of nowhere and covering Merle's body with his own. Another shot and Sarge went still.

Reuben was stunned when he looked back over his shoulder and saw his two loyal companions lying on the edge of the battlefield, lifeless, but he could not retreat to them. He and the remaining soldiers of G Company were advancing to their next objective, Dog Hill 921. Reuben reassured himself; the medics would be there in no time and take Merle and Sarge to the

Army hospital. They would be all right. Then he went down, and everything went black.

# Chapter 26

The success of the 10<sup>th</sup> Mountain Divisions' attack on "Riva Ridge" made the headlines of the *New York Times* and from there spread to newspapers all over the country. "Elite Soldiers," Blue-Blood Troops," "Alpine Division." These words now described the famous "Mountain Infantry." There was a large detailed article printed in the *Blakely Eagle* that Irene and Margaret read with earnest. Now they had a clearer picture of just what was going on over there in Italy. It made Irene proud that her husband was part of such a successful mission but at the same time afraid for him and what lay ahead for him. She bought six newspapers, cut out the articles, and mailed them to Kitty, Lucille, Evelyn, Francis, and Mrs. Hubert. Then she placed the sixth one in her dresser drawer underneath her gold locket.

Her Austin friends in turn sent the write-ups from their local papers to her and she gobbled up every word. Just reading them made her feel closer to Merle, like she was there with him. Along with the newspaper clippings, each of her friends updated Irene on their lives and conditions. Mrs. Hubert had a whole house full of new tenants, but none was as great as Irene and Merle, she said. Kitty's pregnancy was coming along fine, but she had to quit smoking, it just made her sick. Irene couldn't imagine Kitty not smoking and laughed thinking that if it weren't for Kitty, she would have never taken up the nasty habit. Lucille was pregnant and staying with her in-laws. She couldn't stand living alone without Reuben. Francis was also expecting. She just found out. The most distressing news was from Evelyn. Her doctor put her on twenty-four-hour bed rest until her child was born. She had two months to go.

After reading the letters from her old friends, Irene once again began to feel sorry for herself. Why was everyone expecting a baby, everyone except her? She certainly tried hard enough, when she and Merle were together. She wondered why she had such bad luck. Maybe there was something wrong with her, physically. She tried to snap out of her self-pity mood, but just couldn't shake it.

"The girls," came into her room. "The mail man came." Grace said and handed the stack of envelopes to her.

"Oh, thanks Grace," Irene said faking a smile.

"Is there any mail from Merle?" Grace asked, already knowing there was.

"I don't know, let me take a look."

"Oh, yes, there are two letters from him. One is postmarked February 14 and the other February 15." Irene genuinely smiled this time. The rest of the mail was just advertisements and bills.

"Oh goody," Shirley remarked. "We want you to be happy again."

"I'm happy, I'm happy, now you two get out of here and clean up for dinner." Irene shooed them and tore open the first letter. The letters didn't reveal anything about where he was or if he was in action or not. Censored, she knew. Nevertheless, it was such a relief just to see his handwriting, knowing he was alive. He told her he loved her and missed her. Suddenly she felt better. They would have plenty of opportunities to make babies, as soon as the war was over. He would return to her as he promised in Austin and they would raise a family and live happily ever after. That was what she always prayed for and prayed for now. Refreshed, Irene hopped off her bed and went to the kitchen to help her mom prepare supper. Her next letter to Merle had a reminiscent tone.

March 1, 1945
R. D. #2
Shawville, PA

My Dearest Merle,

Here it is the first day of March and here it came in like a lamb. I suppose it will go out like a lion. How is it where you are honey? Is it getting nice there? I hope so, for I don't want you to be out in the cold. I'm awful glad you aren't living out doors, babe. But you said you don't have a very soft bed. Well darling, if you had stayed home here with me, you would have a nice soft bed. Remember how soft it is. We had lots of good sleeps on that old bed, didn't we honey. Shirley sleeps with me now. But I'd rather have you. See I like you. You are my darling and I like you and want you home with me.

We had a letter from Eddie yesterday and he is coming home next week. We will sure be glad to see him. Vince won't get home until later on, about the first of April. And when are you coming home sweetheart? Sometimes I have a notion to join the WACS's. What would you say honey if I did? You wouldn't be mad, would you?

How's Clell? I heard from Evelyn last week. Everyone here is fine. I'm going to send you another box. I did send two, but you probably didn't get them yet. I'm sorry you don't have any beer or whiskey. I surely would send you some if I only could. But I guess I can't.

I sure hope the weather clears up, so I can get me a job soon. I haven't been spending much money though.

I got a letter from Kitty today. I sure was glad to hear from her. She said that Paul had seen you one day, and he told her how bad you felt about your dad. I know darling you must have. I only wish I could have been with you my darling when you got that news. I know I could have made it easier for you Merle if you were home when it happened.

We were at Bingo in Shawville tonight and just got home. That's why I'm up so late writing to you. Mom won fifteen dollars, but I wasn't lucky at all. I hate bingo! I won two free tickets for next week, but I feel sure I'm not going to go.

I got two letters from you yesterday. I hope I get another. I wish you could tell me what you are doing over there. After all of the news here, I finally have an idea.

Young Victor Riley is in this battle; I think it's called Iwo Jeoma. I guess that was a bad battle. Guess what, old Harry Barron from The Mill is across now. I don't know just where. Let's hope you don't run into him. You might just shoot him on the spot. Just kidding.

Well honey, I'm sleepy now so I'd better get to bed. I wish you were here to go to bed with me Merle. That would be fun. If I only had you back I'd be so very happy.

Good Night My Sweet
All My Love And Kisses
Your Own Irene

Margaret came into the living room to see Irene sitting in a chair looking out the window at the rain pouring down. "What are you going to do tonight Reeny? It is Saturday night. Do you want to go to bingo?"

"No, I don't want to go to bingo. I'm going to go to confession to prepare for church tomorrow, as I always do." Irene snapped back. Then feeling badly, she said in a kinder voice, "Have you heard anymore news about Vince? Is he still sick?"

"Nothing new, but Eddie is supposed to arrive home any day now. His furlough came through and he will be home for nine days. All I can say is he had better spend that time here with us instead of with "that girl.""

"Mom, I don't know why you call her "that girl" when he's been seeing Sis for years now. I think they love each other."

"I suppose, but I just think he could do better." Margaret finally revealed her true feelings.

"Just like I could have done better than Merle?"

"It's not that, I just want what is best for my children."

"Well, maybe you don't really know what's best." Irene retorted and decided to drop the subject. "I'm sorry Mom. I'm so worried about Merle. Here it is March already and the last letter I got from him was dated February 15.

Margaret showed her rare softer side and said, "Don't worry Reeny, you know how bungled the military mail is. I'm sure you'll hear from him soon." Irene just nodded, and she returned her gaze out the window at the rain.

The next day, before Mass, Irene took extra time and fixed Grace and Shirley's hair in long spiral curls. She had each of them sit on the kitchen table as she wound the hair around her finger and then secured them with bobby pins. When all of the curls were in place, she put a barrette in the front pulling the hair off their faces. "The girls," looked adorable dressed in their best dresses as they all prayed in church for the end of the war.

Irene was anxious for Monday to come when mail delivery would resume. She longed desperately for word from Merle. Unfortunately, there was no letter on Monday. Irene showed her anger by shaking her fists at the mailbox and growling under her breath. "Grrrrr, I'm mad." She said to no one, just herself as she sulked back through the muddy lane back into the house. Since Irene refused to accompany her mother to bingo, Margaret tried another tactic to cheer her up. "There's a good movie playing in Shawville tomorrow night at the theater. It's called "I Love A Soldier."

Irene perked up and said, "I've heard of that movie. Merle told me about it. Some of it is about Camp Hale in Colorado, where he was stationed."

"Yes, that's the one. Why don't we take "the girls" to see it?"

"Okay." Irene agreed. It was something for her to look forward to, since the mailman continued to disappoint her.

Finally, the next day, on March 7, there was a solitary letter in the mailbox. It was from Merle, written on February 22, nearly three weeks ago. It temporarily eased Irene's worries and fears. She began to cheer up, anxious to see Eddie, expected to arrive late that night.

Eddie came bounding in the door after midnight in uniform and he sure looked good. He resembled their dad, handsome and tall with the same square build. He had matured while he was away and looked much older than his nineteen years. They were all waiting up for him, even Grace and Shirley. The first thing he did was drop the heavy army duffle bag onto the kitchen floor. Then he scooped up "the girls" kissing them more than they kissed him. Then he went to Margaret and hugged her tight and said, "I missed you Mom." He then saw Irene waiting patiently for her turn at his affections and he reached out saying, "Reeny, I'm so glad to be home." They stayed up half the night talking. After "the girls" went to bed, and after drinking six beers, he revealed to

Margaret and Irene how miserable he was in this dam army. He told stories of mistreatment by the Sergeants and by the time he finished his last bottle, referred to them as "dogs." Margaret was sizzling mad that anyone would treat her son that way. The last thing Eddie said before going to bed was, "They made me pack everything I owned to carry home with me on furlough. That bag must weigh one hundred pounds." Irene tried to pick it up and could barely move it.

The time Eddie was home went by like a whirlwind with get togethers and parties taking place practically every night. All the activity helped Irene not to concentrate on the fact that she hadn't received any mail from Merle for weeks. Eddie left on March 15, his destination, Fort Meade and from there, everyone knew he was going over. Irene became extremely lonesome and blue. The March rains continued, Eddie was gone, Vince was still sick in an army hospital and she still hadn't heard from Merle. The news on the radio reported of Allies fighting in Italy. Irene worried and prayed to God to keep him safe. Irene and Margaret's animosity toward each other subsided. Now that Margaret realized how bad the soldiers had it, she was no longer angry with Irene for leaving them and spending time with Merle in Austin. Irene kept writing everyday even though she got nothing in return and she tried to keep her letters positive and hopeful. She tried.

Shawville, PA
March 19, 1945

Dearest Merle,

Hello darling, how's my boy today? I hope fine and dandy. It's still raining here and very dreary. It has rained practically every day this month, just like it rained or snowed every time I ever left you, even in Texas. I feel so lonesome for you I don't know what to do.

Boy, when you do land home, you had better give me a good loving up honey. I think I'll kiss you to pieces. I think I'll have to have about a hundred kisses before I ever stop. So, don't forget, I'll be disappointed if I don't get them sweetheart.

I think this is a hell of an old war. I sure hope and pray it gets over soon and you are home again for I really do miss you.

We haven't heard from Vince for about six weeks. I think he is out of the hospital now. I guess he was pretty sick.

I was over to church this morning. I went to confession last night and went to communion this morning. It is St. Joseph's Day and that is a big day at our church. I prayed that you are safe, and Merle be safe honey, and I feel sure if I keep up my faith that you are all right, you will be. You keep your trust in God too that everything will turn out okay for us. We've had so much trouble already, but sometime soon, it's bound to change sweetheart.

Well, my darling, I guess I will hurry and mail this now for the mailman will be here soon now. I'm keeping my fingers crossed so he has a letter from you for me.

Well sweetie darling, I must say bye now. I love you more and more and sweet, keep your chin up and pray, and I'll do the same for you.

Love, Luck and Lots of
Kisses
Your Wife

She stuck her last three-cent stamp on the envelope, pulled on her boots and coat and slopped through the mud to the mailbox, opened it up, tossed the letter inside and lifted the flag. By now, she was soaked despite her raingear but didn't hurry back inside. The mailman pulled up right before she reached the house. Irene turned her head expectantly only to see him shaking his head toward her, indicating there was no letter. She hung her head and burst into tears.

Inside, she shed her wet coat and muddy boots and retreated to her room. Irene crawled into her bed and pulled the covers over her head. She closed her eyes and tried to escape from the world. At some time, she fell asleep. Suppertime came and went. Margaret told "the girls" to let Reeny sleep. She needed it. Later there was a knock at the door. Grace was doing her homework at the kitchen table and Shirley was drawing pictures, sitting across from Grace. Margaret opened the door. "Irene Heasley?" the man asked.

"No, I'm her mother. Who are you?" Margaret took a closer look through the dark and realized the man at the door was in uniform, an army uniform, and close behind him was another, dressed the same.

"We need to speak to Irene Heasley." The second soldier responded. "Is she here?" Shirley slid off the kitchen chair and inched closer to her mom and the strangers at the door. She grabbed hold of her mother's skirt and peeked around her at the men. Grace looked up from her homework more annoyed at the interruption than curious.

"Yes, she is here, just a minute." Margaret settled Shirley back into the kitchen chair and went to Irene's bedroom. She shook Irene awake and told her she had visitors at the door. A groggy, barefooted Irene made her way to the door. Pushing her hair out of her face, she tried to focus on the two men. She could barely make out their faces in the fog that now accompanied the rain.

"Irene Heasley?" The soldier asked again.

"Yes, I'm Irene, what do you want?"

"We are deeply sorry to have to tell you, your husband, Merle Heasley, was killed in action near C. Romito, Italy, in the line of duty on March 3." The uniformed man looked down and handed her a telegram stating the same.

Irene screamed, "No, no, no. It has to be a mistake. I've been praying for him. He's not dead." She rushed out the door past the soldiers and started running, running toward the bridge shoeless, slipping, and falling in the mud. She picked herself up and continued running. She ran the whole way to the bridge where she collapsed against the wooden railing sobbing uncontrollably.

Shirley, now hysterical, shouted, "Grace, Reeny is running toward the bridge. She can't go near the bridge at night. It's rainy and foggy, just like the night old Sadie disappeared. Reeny is going to die, just like old Sadie and never be heard from again."

Grace, realizing the seriousness of the visitors at the door, tried to calm Shirley down. Margaret was pulling on her boots and coat ready to go after Irene when they saw her walking back toward the house, obviously broken. The soldiers again offered their condolences and left the doorstep. Margaret gathered Irene in her arms and took her to the bathroom, put her in the bathtub and washed the mud from her body and her hair. Shirley settled down as soon as she saw Reeny was back and "the girls" comforted each other that night, knowing Merle would never be back. He would never tease Shirley again saying he was going to bite her on her Adam's apple. He would never carry Grace around on his shoulders again galloping like a horse. He would never be back.

# Chapter 27

Surveillance reports indicated there were approximately eighty thousand Japanese soldiers stationed on Okinawa as well as over five hundred thousand civilians. The bombardment in preparation of the strike on the island was complete. On Sunday, April 1, 1945, just as strategically planned, the amphibious landing commenced. The United States Army invaded the southern part of the sixty-five-mile island and the United States Marines assaulted the north. Early on, word had spread to the crew of The *Alaska* that the Army had advanced four miles and had captured three airfields. Ross gave a thumbs up to his fellow engine room companions, but he was more concerned about the storm that was coming their way. The weather radio had been warning the ships involved in the Okinawa invasion that a typhoon would hit them within twenty-four hours. Despite the warnings, their support of the ground troops on Okinawa continued and on April 2, the Navy's torpedo boats got one Japanese cruiser and one tin can. Other forces destroyed four small torpedo boats.

When they could delay no longer, the big ships sustaining the Okinawa battle took evasive action to get out of the path of the huge storm bearing down upon them. The *Alaska* changed its course to the south, trying to get as close as they could to the Philippines. On the morning of April 3, they suffered the wrath of the storm. It was impossible to control the ship with one hundred and twenty miles per hour winds rocking them and the rains beating at them. The huge carrier rolled back and forth and everything topside tore loose. Lifelines and powder cans were ripped right off the deck. During the typhoon, they almost rammed another carrier, but just missed. Ross was thinking, just our luck, we survived Kamikaze plane attacks only to be killed by a typhoon. They survived the deluge.

On April 5, in the aftermath of the typhoon, The *Alaska* relieved the Australian Royal Navy, one of the United States' closest allies, just north of Formosa and South of Okinawa. One of the Limeys, shouted to the sailors topside of The *Alaska*, "Be on the lookout for Japanese suicide planes. We lost a carrier to one of them."

"Thanks for the warning," The Americans yelled back "We are going home for some recreation."

"Go ahead, we will fight the war." The *Alaska* crewmembers joked.

They waved and steamed away shouting, "Tally Ho."

Only two days after this encounter, *Alaska*'s carrier planes were attacking Japanese surface units that were moving through the East China Sea toward Okinawa. They were successful in sinking the giant battleship, The *Yamoto*. Also destroyed were 2 cruisers and 3 cans. The *Alaska* was about one hundred miles east of the ships when the planes attacked them. Operating off Okinawa and Kyushu, *Alaska*'s guns protected the fast carriers in the task force, which sent daily sweeps of "Hellcats" over enemy airfields, shore installations, and shipping ports.

The only break for Ross Kepple and the crew was on April 10 when they pulled out of the area to refuel. Then they were told the time-line for taking Okinawa would be at least three or four more months. Ross didn't think he could take it much longer. There was nothing to look forward to and he was scared and sick of being on the ship. To the surprise of everyone on the ship, they got mail that day. Delivered to Ross was a small stack of letters and one box. Finally, he had something to take his thoughts away from the constant firing of guns. There were letters from his brother and Jeannie. The box was from his mom. Inside was a jar of Mohawk Valley Limburger Cheese, a gift for his birthday. The note inside said, "Ross, I know your birthday is over a month away, but I wanted to make sure you got this in time and I know how much you love Limburger. Be safe. Love, Mom, and Dad."

The next day they were right back in action again. *Alaska* assisted in shooting down a Japanese plane and shot another one down unassisted. In the midst of the chaos, the captain announced to them that President Roosevelt had died at 3:35 pm on April 12 in his home state of Georgia and now former vice president Harry Truman would be running the show. The sailors didn't know what to think about that. Would Truman be up to the task to finish this war? They all prayed that he was.

# Chapter 28

Even though Grace and Shirley realized Merle wouldn't be coming back, Irene refused to believe it. She was convinced it was a mistake and she would soon see the soldiers at her door with another telegram apologizing to her for making such an error. Margaret was at her wits end as what to do with her. They talked, fought, and cried for days, but Irene was in complete denial. She began to write letters to Merle's comrades in the 10th Mountain Division that she had met in Austin for confirmation of her beliefs. Irene hastily wrote desperate letters to Clell, Reuben, Mel, and Paul and anyone reading them would be convinced a mad woman wrote them. She also wrote to their wives searching for any information to verify the gigantic mistake the Army had made.

April 1, 1945
California, PA

Dearest Irene,
I hardly know how to write this letter. There is very little I can do or say to you at this particular time. You know my heartaches for you, but please don't give up hope that Merle is alive.

Clell was wounded sometime between February 24 and March 3. He wrote and told me it wasn't serious, then I got word from the War Department he was making normal improvement with a penetrating wound in the forehead. I got a letter from him today and he is sending me a Purple Heart and they have taken out the stitches. He will be fighting again very soon.

Irene, it certainly was a shock to me to know Clell was wounded, but I don't know what I would have done if I had gotten a visit and telegram like you.

Thank God, Irene, you and I stayed in Texas. We will always have those memories of the wonderful times we had there.

Irene, I'm so disgusted with this war I could scream. It doesn't let up a bit. All this country can do is take kids and send them over there and draft married men with four and five kids in the family. I think this country is going war crazy.

I am going to write to Clell and ask him to find out anything he can for us about Merle. I know if anyone can find out for certain, Clell will.

The doctor says I am still getting along all right. I only have about one more month to go. If I get any more shocks, I don't know what will happen.

Why don't you come down to see me? The change will do you good. I sincerely hope and pray the telegram was wrong. Don't give up.

Your friend,
Evelyn

Evelyn's letter only made Irene surer of her conviction that the notification delivered by the soldiers was a slip-up. Margaret and "the girls," were so worried about Reeny, but they still didn't know what to do. When the last letters Irene sent to Merle began returning, Margaret was sure she would come to her senses. A red stamp shaped like a pointing hand with the words "Return to Sender," marred the front of each envelope. The hand-written word "Deceased" was scrawled underneath the stamp on all seventeen of them and the mailman delivered them daily. Irene would just stuff them in her drawer unopened along with all of the other letters she had received from Merle over the last two years. It wasn't until she received a reply from Reuben Painter that things changed.

April 11, 1945
Italy

Dear Irene,
Just a few lines to let you know I received your letter concerning Merle. I really can't tell you a heck of a lot, but I'll do my best.
I know it would be hard to believe something like that. It's too dam bad something like this has to happen in our families.

Irene, I'm sure you won't get a letter telling you it was a mistake because I was with him. It happened very quick; he didn't know anything about it and Sarge went with him. It wasn't long after that until I got it, but I'm doing okay. I hope to be out of this place soon.

I just want you to remember the good times we all had together in Austin and ever since we left there, all Merle did was talk about you. It was really nice of you to spend the time you could there before Merle went overseas. I'm sure you will never regret it a bit.

I guess it was pretty blue on his mother, two deaths in the family in such a short period of time.

My wife, Lucille, said in her last letter she was writing to you, but it is hard for her to write to you in a case like this especially in her condition. She doesn't want to do anything to upset herself while she is expecting.

Well, I had better close for this time. If you feel you want to keep in touch with us, feel free to do so. May God bless you and watch over you at all times, and best of luck.

Sincerely,
Reuben

P.S. Please excuse my writing or spelling. I'm as nervous as a ninety-year-old man.

Irene could deny the truth no longer, not after reading Reuben's letter. She looked up from the pencil scribbled words to see her mom and "the girls" looking at her, waiting for some signal as to what she read. Irene reached out to them and said, "I'm sorry. I'm so sorry for putting you all through this these past weeks. I know now that Merle is gone, killed in action in Italy, just like the soldier's telegram said." Two widows and two young girls hugged each other, not another word was spoken about the denials of the past few weeks.

By the end of April, Merle's body arrived home and a Purple Heart came a few days later. After a funeral Mass, Irene buried him beside his father, behind the old log church. There were no more emotional outbursts by Irene, no more tears. She had no reaction to the death of President Roosevelt; she was numb to what was going around her in the world. She went into a trance, going through the motions of life without any joy, just existing and wearing black. Grace and Shirley tried to bring Irene out of her depression with lively conversation. "When I grow up, I want to be a nurse." Grace cheerfully said to Irene.

Shirley smiled and replied, "I want to be a nurse too."

Irene glanced at the two of them and replied in a monotone voice, "Girls, life is but an empty dream. There is no utopia." Then she walked out of the house and sauntered up the lane looking down at her feet.

"I want the old Reeny back." Shirley wailed.

"So do I Shirley, but I don't think she will ever be the old Reeny again." Grace said.

# Chapter 29

The soldiers of the 10th Mountain Division pushed forward in April 1945 carrying out their objectives, without Merle Heasley. They broke the German's mountain line and crossed the Po River. By the end of the month, they encountered little resistance. The 10th completely destroyed five elite German divisions. After over one hundred days of combat, the 10th Division suffered casualties of nine hundred and ninety-two killed in action and four thousand one hundred and fifty-four wounded. This time the five young soldiers who bonded in Austin were part of the statistics.

The Allies were having the same success all over Europe defeating the enemy and the German army was in tatters. Finally, the last German forces were trapped between the Allies advancing from France and from Russia. On April 30, Adolf Hitler committed suicide in his Berlin bunker. On May 7, Germany signed unconditional surrender documents. It was five years, eight months and six days since Hitler began his Nazi scourge. It would take effect at one minute after midnight. The war in Europe was officially over on May 8, 1945. The day of Victory in Europe was suitably shortened to V-E Day.

The streets of cities all over the world filled with yelling, whistling people celebrating the end of German occupation in Europe. Main Street in Blakely was no exception. Cars stopped wherever they were, and their drivers leaned on their horns adding to the pandemonium.

The new President Truman's radio address proclaimed complete and final victory in the European theater of the greatest war in history. His radio address solemnly warned, "Our victory is but half won. The west is free, but the east is still in bondage to the treacherous tyranny of the Japanese. When the last Japanese division has surrendered unconditionally, only then will our fighting job be done." In Truman's proclamation, he designated the following Sunday, Mother's Day, as a day of prayer. He asked, "All Americans to give thanks to God for the victory we have won and to pray for support to the end our present struggle and guide us into the way of peace."

Irene turned off the radio and went into the kitchen sulking about the way her life had turned out. She refused to go to church since Merle died. Her excuse was God didn't care about her. He never answered her millions of prayers. Prayers to have a baby, prayers to save her dad, prayers to protect Merle, none of them were answered. She quit praying.

After the President's radio address, Margaret approached Irene and said, "Honey, I think it's time you go back to church. The president has made this Sunday as a day of prayer. You are going to church with us this Sunday." She demanded.

Irene glared at her saying, "God doesn't care if I go to church or not. He doesn't care about me at all."

"Reeny, you know that is not true. Everything happens for a reason. We just can't understand why bad things happen, but when they do, you must keep your faith for that is all we really have."

"God just causes me pain. I'm better off not thinking about him or praying to him, it's easier that way."

"Life is not supposed to be easy. How do you think I felt when at twelve years old, everyone I ever loved was dead, but I didn't give up?" Margaret revealed feelings never said. "At least you still have Grace and Shirley and your brothers and me."

On Sunday, May 13, Irene accompanied Margaret and "the girls," to Mass at St. Josephs. She prayed once again to her God that had given her so many disappointments in life. She had to.

# Chapter 30

Finally, the Pacific theater would get the attention it was waiting for. The exuberant soldiers celebrating V-E Day packed their duffels and headed to the Pacific where the Battle of Okinawa was still going on strong. Reinforcements would finally arrive to strengthen the battle-weary sailors.

The *Alaska* was anchored at Ulithi to be overhauled where the men got some recreation after a long tour of almost two months. They celebrated the end of the war in Europe their own way. Each man, allotted three bottles of beer, downed them on the ninety-degree island of Mog Mog.

Ross Kepple celebrated his twenty-fifth birthday on Mog Mog. He and his friends stole a loaf of bread from the ship's baker and they had Mohawk Valley Limburger cheese sandwiches and beers on the sandy beach. On May 24, after ten days in Ulithi, they were underway for Okinawa again. *Alaska* sailed as part of the 3rd Fleet with Task Group 38.4. Two new ships joined their formation, the battleship *Iowa* and the carrier *Ticonderoga*. They once again screened a portion of the fast carrier task force. Admiral Halsey, in charge of the 3rd Fleet, was commanding from the *Missouri*, also in their unit.

Early in June, all night gunfire lit up the horizon from the battleship's continual bombardment of Okinawa. Carrier planes from The *Alaska* hit Kyushu and her cans exploded a floating mine, only one hundred yards starboard of them. *Alaska* and her sister ship, *Guam*, shelled the Japanese held Okino Diato Shima, just south of Minami Daito Shimo. They destroyed the enemy radar sites discovered there. On June 14, The *Alaska* arrived in San Pedro Bay, Leyte, in the Philippine Islands for another overhaul. While there, the captain announced over the intercom that Okinawa had been captured. Cheers echoed from all quarters. Rumors circulated around the ship that they would be picking up soldiers in Leyte that just arrived there from Europe. They would be instrumental in the completion of their next mission, the attack of Southern Japan.

A platoon of one hundred army soldiers boarded The *Alaska* in Leyte geared up and prepared to take on the Japanese, feeling confident after overthrowing Hitler. Ross watched as the weary platoon marched on deck loaded down with equipment. Their already cramped quarters would only be more uncomfortable now that they had to accommodate one hundred more men.

Among the new passengers was Eddie Taft. He certainly didn't want any part of attacking Japan, but he thought it couldn't be any worse than fighting under Patton. Eddie left home back in March for Fort Meade, Maryland, and from there he went overseas to Italy. After V-E Day, he was sent to the Leyte Gulf and was now on board The *Alaska*. He no sooner boarded the ship than he got sick. Over half of the crew was sick too. Stomach cramps and diarrhea were the symptoms. It was determined the water onboard was polluted, a result of too many ships anchored in the gulf depositing waste into the waters. After chlorine was put in the drinking water, symptoms subsided. Before Eddie's condition worsened, he admitted himself into sickbay. The hospital ward on the ship was full and the smell was atrocious. While recovering, Eddie thought he recognized one of the other victims of polluted water. He said to his friend, "What are the odds of me knowing anyone onboard this ship?"

"You have two odds, slim and none." Parker, his best friend, said.

"But that guy looks so familiar." Eddie responded, not ready to give up on it.

"Go ask him his name. That will be the end of it."

"He looks pretty miserable. I don't want to bother him now." The chlorine did the trick and within a few days, the ship left Leyte headed for a new advanced base near recently captured Okinawa. Eddie saw the same sailor topside while they were off Okinawa and took a closer look. Yes, he looked like the guy from Shawville that was after his sister Irene, years ago. He was sure it was him. Eddie approached him on deck. "How's it going sailor?" he began.

The sailor looked at him cautiously, "It's going." Ross Kepple didn't trust anyone anymore, something he learned in the Navy.

"Where are you from?" asked Eddie.

"Pennsylvania. Why?" the sailor answered.

"I'm from Pennsylvania too, from a little town near Pittsburgh." Eddie said, even more sure of his convictions.

"What town?" asked Ross.

"Shawville, well, about six miles outside of Shawville, between Blakely and Shawville."

"I'm from Shawville too, right in town." Ross said.

"I knew it, I knew it from the first time I saw you in sickbay. You're the guy from Shawville who was sneaking around seeing my sister, Reeny, back in '41 before this dam war started." Eddie accusingly said while looking him straight in the eye.

Ross's thoughts raced through his head having trouble recognizing this young man but clearly remembering Reeny and he felt his heart skip a beat just at the sound of her name.

"You mean, Irene, Irene Taft. Then you must be Eddie. You got so tall. I would have never recognized you. You're little Eddie Taft, aren't you?"

"Yes, I'm Ed Taft." He said, preferring a less childish name now.

Ross was so taken back he couldn't speak. He looked at Eddie in disbelief that here he was in the Pacific, in the middle of war, having this conversation with Reeny's little brother. He had spent the last four years trying to get Irene out of his head and now all the thoughts and memories of her came flooding back. After what must have been too long, he said, "How is Irene, and "the girls," and Margaret?"

Ross knew, just by the look on Eddie's face, something was wrong. "What is it?" he asked. "What, are they all right?" he persisted.

Eddie said, "What is your name anyhow? I never did know. All I knew back then was, Reeny was smitten by you, and then you disappeared from her life. You broke her heart."

"My name is Ross, Ross Kepple. What do you mean I broke her heart? I wrote her a letter before going out on patrol, but never heard back from her. I thought she didn't want me bothering her. I knew she had a boyfriend, so I let it go."

"Oh yes, I remember the day she got your letter. Mom even hid it from Merle and Dad. She got your letter all right and then the letter she sent to you came back in the mail, return to sender, address unknown. She checked the mailbox every day for months hoping for another letter from you, but none ever came."

While all of this was sinking in, Ross repeated, "Is she okay?"

"Well, no. I would imagine she's in a bad way right now."

"What do you mean?"

"Do you want to hear the long version or the short version?"

"I want to hear it all, you see, I fell in love with her back then even though we only had three weeks together. I never stopped thinking about Irene, all of these years."

Eddie, feeling better about Ross Kepple, told the story. "Well, I'll give you the short version.

Reeny and Merle got married right after the attack on Pearl Harbor and in '43 he got drafted into the Army. He trained in camps all over the States but right before he went over; he was stationed at Camp Swift in Texas. That was when Reeny left home and went to Austin to be with him. Boy was Mom mad at her for leaving her and "the girls" all alone."

"Where was your dad?" Ross asked.

"Oh, I left that part out." Eddie looked down holding back the emotions he got when he thought about his dad. "Dad died from injuries in a car wreck about a year before." Eddie slowly added.

"Go on." Ross said dying to hear more.

"When the 10th Mountain Division got their orders they were going overseas, Reeny came home from Texas. Mom, Reeny, Grace, and Shirley were all living together since, oh I'd say last December in Reeny and Merle's house."

"Did you say the 10th Mountain Division?"

"Yes, that was Merle's division and they were sent to Italy to fight in the mountains."

Ross said, "I read all about the 10th fighting the Germans in Italy. Irene's husband was part of that group?" He was picturing the drunk Merle Heasley passed out at the bar of Mrs. Carlotta's at his birthday party so many years ago and couldn't imagine that man part of an elite fighting force. He kept his thoughts to himself and prodded Eddie to continue.

"I was home on furlough just this past March and at that time Reeny hadn't heard from Merle for weeks. She still had no news when I left. She was worried sick."

"What ever happened to your brother? Vince, was that his name?"

"Vince was drafted into the Navy. He is over here somewhere. I don't know exactly where, but I don't think he's too far from us."

Their conversation had to end there. Ross was late for his shift in the engine room and he dared not delay getting to his post any longer. "Ed, I have to go, but let's meet tomorrow. I really want to talk to you some more."

Eddie gave him a wave and then vomited over the railing. He didn't have his sea legs yet and the rocking ship made him sick.

Ross searched for Eddie the next day and finally spotted him at chow time and sat down beside him. Eddie wasn't eating much; his stomach was still unsettled from the seasickness that over took him. "Hello again," Ross said and sat down beside him digging into his rations. Eddie took a small bite of food and looked over at him nodding, acknowledging his presence. He didn't feel up to talking right now. "What did you mean when you said Irene was in a bad way right now?"

Eddie forced himself to swallow and then said, "On Leyte, just before I boarded ship, we had mail call. I got a letter from Mom. She wrote that Merle was killed in action in Italy in early March. The soldiers delivered the telegram to Reeny, but she refused to believe it and was acting like a crazy person. She didn't accept it until she got a letter from the soldier who was with him when he died, someone she knew from Austin. So, I imagine, she's still in a bad way."

Suddenly, Ross didn't feel like eating either. He dropped his fork and just stared ahead.

# Chapter 31

Amidst the sympathy cards that filled the mailbox, Irene received a birth notice from Evelyn. Clell Wesley Hughey was born on May 4, 1945. His eyes were blue, his hair was brown, and he weighed eight and one-half pounds. Evelyn invited Irene to come down to visit and see "little junior." It would be good for her and help her get over her loss, she said. Margaret, this time agreed knowing Irene needed a change of scenery. "Irene, Merle has been gone for nearly two months now. You need to get on with your life. I think visiting your old friend is a great idea."

"Okay Mom, I'll go, even though I don't want to." Irene reluctantly agreed. She decided she would only stay for one night and packed accordingly. After she got there, she was glad for the short stay. Little Clell was cute but he cried incessantly. Evelyn did everything she knew to do to comfort him, but nothing worked. Irene tried to give poor Evelyn a break, but it didn't help at all. The day Irene departed from California, Pennsylvania, Evelyn took her new baby boy to the hospital emergency room.

The following week, Irene received a letter from Evelyn's mother telling her that the baby had died. Irene knew there was something wrong with him, but she couldn't pinpoint what it was. Her heart ached for Evelyn, and her husband, who never even saw his son. Merle's good friend, Clell, was in Italy when the baby was born and headed for the Pacific when he died. For the first time in months, Irene was feeling sorry for someone other than herself.

The old adage, time heals, is certainly true. As time went by, Irene slowly came back into the real world. She even accompanied her mom to bingo, on occasion. Grace and Shirley were especially happy to have the old Reeny back…almost. "The girls" went to the Danville School, the same one room school Irene went to until eighth grade. Shirley, now ten years old was always breaking the rules just to see if she could get away with it and Grace always came to her defense and covered up for her sister's devilish behavior. Irene kept her cigarettes in her purse hidden away from "the girls," but the day Shirley and four other kids were sent home from school because they were caught smoking on the playground, Irene checked her purse and her cigarettes were gone. Not only was Shirley in trouble at school, she became violently ill. It turned out she also found an old can of snuff hidden in Reeny's car. She shared the snuff with the other kids and they swallowed it. Margaret was embarrassed and furious at Shirley.

Fortunately, for Shirley, summer vacation came soon, and her trouble was forgotten.

Money was a major concern for Irene now that Merle had died. She did receive a nice amount of money from his government insurance policy, but it would not sustain her forever. She put it under her mattress and tried not to spend it. She knew she had to go back to work now. She had no choice. The Mill reinstated her, and she was lucky to get her old job back delivering mail throughout the plant. Irene couldn't believe how her life had changed, but ironically remained the same. In a relatively short period of time, she buried her father, quit her job, and traveled to Austin to spend time with her husband, and since buried her husband and was now back at The Mill, doing the same job.

Margaret was worried about survival too. She knew Irene should not be responsible for supporting her and "the girls" and decided to change her life too. Frank Taft was dead now, over a year, and she was only forty-five years old, not too old to find someone else to take care of her. Margaret stopped wearing black and now dressed in bright colors. She got her hair done at the beauty parlor every week. Margaret put on makeup and took pleasure in spraying on perfume. Her favorite was the "Yellow Rose of Texas," the gift Irene gave her. Her social life consisted mostly of her friends at the bingo halls. She was always dressed to the hilt, her hair, and make up perfect, when she strolled inside the halls and took her seat. After touching up her lipstick and placing her pocket book on the chair next to her, she would buy twelve cards, light up a cigarette and set the stage for the kill. It was uncanny, but she was lucky and won often. The other players took notice of her luck, especially one player who had been watching and admiring her for months. He was a widower and he intentionally took a chair across from her on every bingo night.

Irene accompanied her mom one night, loathing having to endure losing her money at this silly game. This night she noticed how the man across the table was smitten with her mother. It was obvious some sort of relationship had developed. Irene was immediately shocked and jealous. Why should her mother be able to attract the attention of a man when she couldn't, not that she wanted to? It was too soon for her to even think about anyone else but Merle. Irene still wore black. She had to for one year, that's what everyone told her.

After Reeny and Margaret got home that night, Irene took a good look at herself in the mirror. She looked pale and too thin. Irene took her hands and pulled her hair back and smiled back at her reflection. She decided at that moment, her destiny was going to change. She was going to pick herself up and stop wallowing in self-pity and carry on with her life. Irene went to bed that night and talked to Merle for the last time. "Merle I loved you and I miss you. Please forgive me, but I have to go on with my life without you. Good-bye." The next day, she hung her black clothes in the back of the closet, too soon for the traditional neighborhood, but she didn't care.

The delicious smell of breakfast cooking woke "the girls" before Reeny could holler to them, "Upstairs maids, it's time to get up." Grace and Shirley couldn't believe their senses. Reeny was back! They raced into the kitchen and found their older sister dressed in a bright yellow dress covered by their mom's apron, cooking bacon and eggs singing, "Life is just a bowl of cherries." She sang the rest of the song while dancing around the kitchen and Shirley and Grace danced right along with her.

# Chapter 32

After talking to Eddie Taft, the first thing Ross wanted to do was write a letter to Irene to let her know he didn't mean to break her heart, tell her he still loved her, and let her know how sorry he was about the loss of her husband, but deep inside, he wasn't sorry. He was glad that he might have another chance to be with her again, after the war. Yes, he would wait until the war was over and then write to her. There was no sense in trying to contact her now. The plans to attack southern Japan took precedence.

Ross heard all the rumors. The attack on Japan would be the bloodiest battle of the Pacific war. The estimation was, hundreds of thousands of allied forces would die, but it was a necessary sacrifice to stop the Japanese and end the war. There was another rumor circulating around the ship, one that bordered upon the unbelievable. The United States had a super bomb that could wipe out Japan completely. The estimated death toll would be in the hundreds of thousands, which would take out everyone, including women and children. Either scenario predicted a horrific death toll. Ross and his fellow sailors, working in the engine room of The *Alaska* just did their jobs, knowing they had no control over the destiny of the world.

On July 10, 1945, the massive bomber raids on Japan began. The *Alaska* sailed again as part of the newly formed Task Force 95. They shelled beaches two hundred and fifty miles north of Tokyo targeting Japanese steel mills. After refueling at Buckner Bay in Okinawa, they were underway for the East China Sea.

Eddie Taft along with most of his comrades that boarded in Leyte were assigned to another ship in the fleet. Ross was able to talk to him one last time before they departed. "Eddie, I would really like to have your sister's address. When this old war is over, I would like to write to her."

Eddie said, "Sure, why not, it might be good for her." He scribbled the address down on a napkin in the mess hall and handed it to him. Ross thanked him and stuffed it in his pocket.

It was not known to the military forces in the Pacific, the super bomb, that was rumored about, was successfully tested in the United States.

The crew of The *Alaska* listened intently when the intercom announced their mission in the East China Sea was to knock out shipping along the China coast, the first patrol of its kind. Unfortunately, their sweep along the China coast was delayed, due to weather. Another typhoon was in their way. After surviving mother nature's forces once again, they continued into the sea and soon realized floating mines surrounded the ship. Suddenly, water filled the engine room. Disaster was diverted when the men surveyed the cause and was able to close the valves to the chamber that was damaged by one of those floating mines. The damage was minimal, and they continued on their mission.

# Chapter 33

President Truman's advisors estimated that an attack on southern Japan would result in 500,000 Japanese casualties and in addition to that, at least 100,000 allied forces would die. While the Air Force, Army, Navy, and the Marines geared up for battle, Truman was praying for an alternative plan.  He really didn't want to have the deaths of 600,000 people on his shoulders.

The day after Roosevelt's death, after he was sworn in as President, Truman's Secretary of War, Henry Stimson, briefed him on the top-secret Manhattan Project. It wasn't until after this briefing he realized there might be another option. Unbeknownst to him, while he was vice president, the war department had been working on developing a super bomb that could wipe out 100,000 people with one drop.  He was not only astounded, but also insulted that such a devastating weapon was being created without the

Vice President of the United States even knowing about it. Now that he knew, it was up to him to follow through on the secret plan to end the war.

It was Truman who approved the order to test the first atomic device on July 16, 1945. The explosion took place at Alamogordo, New Mexico under extreme secrecy. The atomic bomb was perfected and by July 26, the most terrible weapon ever known in human history was shipped to Tinian Island in the South Pacific, the pre-determined launch point. He could only pray he was making the right decision for the United States and the world.

# Chapter 34

The latest news from the WOSR radio was the Allies were winning the war and the conflict in the Pacific would soon be over. This was certainly welcome news for Margaret Taft. She worried incessantly about Vince and Eddie who were over there somewhere. Things did improve for the Taft women especially since Reeny came to her senses regarding Merle's death, but Margaret was a little concerned about the way Irene was acting lately.

Irene would go to work every day at The Mill and after work she always met her girlfriends at the new popular bar in Blakely, The Manhattan. More often than not, she would come home a little tipsy. Margaret was hoping this was just a passing phase and let it go.

The last letter she got from Eddie relieved her worries a bit. He was on a ship in the Pacific with his longtime friend, Parker, and they were okay. He wrote that he ran into someone on the ship from Shawville. It was that guy who was trying to steal Reeny from Merle a long time ago. He told her Ross Kepple asked for Reeny's address and he gave it to him.

Margaret kept this to herself for a while, then one day decided to fill Irene in on the news. It was mid-August and they were getting "the girls" ready to go to the church picnic when she said, "Reeny I got a letter from Eddie the other day."

"Oh, how is he doing?" Reeny asked.

"He is good and still with Parker. They are on a ship in the Pacific." Margaret paused to see if Reeny was paying attention. She wasn't sure if she was or not, but went on, "Yes, he met a sailor on the ship that is from Shawville, right in town."

Irene started to pay attention now and looked at her mom and said, "Really, what are the odds of that happening? Did Eddie know him, what was his name?"

Margaret was slow to reply, but then said, "Well he sort of knew him, he knew who he was."

"Who was it?" Irene demanded to know.

"It was Ross Kepple, that sailor that you were seeing from Shawville, back before the war."

Irene's response was not what Margaret expected. "Oh, him. I'm not going to go through that again." She finished up fixing Shirley's hair and moved on to Grace's obviously annoyed by the news. After having a wonderful time at the picnic and eating too much food, they came home, and all got ready for bed. It was only then, lying in bed that Irene allowed herself to remember, remember the short time they spent together, and how much fun they had and how she fell in love with him. Then she remembered the pain of her heartbreak after losing touch with him. She decided, now that Merle was gone, she had to try to contact him, but how? She decided she would write to Eddie the next morning, maybe he could help.

# Chapter 35

President Truman was ready, he was tired of all the death and destruction and wanted no more of it. He only had one choice. Drop the bomb on Japan.

On August 6, 1945 Truman gave the order for the deadly "Super Bomb" to be to be loaded aboard a B-29 bomber called *Enola Gay*. The bomb was called "Little Boy" and it was dropped by parachute over Hiroshima, Japan around 8:15 a.m. Hiroshima was a manufacturing city with a population near 350,000 and it was 500 miles from Tokyo. These are reasons it was selected as the first target. The bomb exploded 2,000 feet above the city destroying everything in sight for miles.

Truman and his war room were expecting immediate surrender from Japan's emperor, but none came.

On August 9, another B-29 bomber, this one named *Boskcar* took off from Tinian heading for

Nagasaki, another populated Japanese city, carrying the plutonium bomb called "Fat Man". It was dropped at 11:00 a.m. once again devastating miles of terrain.

Over 100,000 Japanese people were immediately killed after the bombings. The Japanese Emperor Hirohito had to surrender, and he did on August 15.

The news of surrender spread unbelievably fast. President Truman and the whole world were relieved and thankful. "Victory in Japan" reduced to "V-J Day" celebrations were held in the United States and in all the other Allied countries.

The official surrender ceremony took place on September 2, 1945 on the USS *Missouri* in Tokyo Bay.

# Chapter 36

The crew of The *Alaska* were told by their Captain that the war was over, but their mission was not. The Japanese had surrendered after the bombings on Hiroshima and Nagasaki. They had no time to celebrate but Ross and the rest of the sailors were so ecstatic that this war and their time at sea was finally coming to an end. There was one more mission before they could go home.

Their last duty was labeled "Magic Carpet". They picked US Army soldiers from Tsingtao China to take them back to the United States.

On September 6, 1945 The *Alaska* was only four miles from the coast of China. Ross was topside, and he was able to see the Great Wall of China. This was his dream since high school and the incredible size of it was more that he could have imagined. He stared at it as long as it was in view and after he could no longer see it, he retreated to his bunk feeling satisfied that this dream was achieved.

The ship was ordered to sail for the United States on November 14, 1945 and stopped once again in Pearl Harbor. After stopping in San Francisco, where the soldiers they were transporting were left off, they proceeded across the Atlantic to the Panama Canal.

They left the Panama Canal and arrived in the Boston Navy Yard on December 18. It was almost Christmas.

Ross was thrilled and surprised to learn that he was to go on an immediate one month leave and would be going home within the week. He thought now is my chance to try to reunite with Reeny. He reached in his pocket and pulled out the wrinkled napkin with her address scribbled on it that Ed gave to him.

Ross wrote her a letter trying to be as thoughtful as possible and put it in the mail.

# Chapter 37

The war was finally over, and life returned to normal, well almost, for the two widows and two little girls living together waiting for news when Vince and Eddie would be coming home.

Irene was disappointed when she got the notice from The Mill that she was no longer needed there. All of the women that were hired to replace the men that were sent off to war were fired, or let go, as they were told. The jobs were for the men returning from the war. Irene liked working at a good job that paid a decent wage and once again was outraged at the injustice, just like not being allowed to go on to high school so long ago. She knew once again, this was all based on her gender. Her last day was on December 20, 1945 and she and her female work friends all met at The Manhattan after work to complain and drink. This made Irene feel better for the short term but in the long term she had to make plans for the future. She focused on her brothers, Vince and Eddie, to see when they would be coming home and anxiously checked the mail daily for news.

One day late in December, Irene emptied the mailbox and flipped through the mail. In it was one letter addressed to her. She quickly ripped it open and to her surprise she read:

December 22, 1945

Dear Irene,

I am not sure, after all this time, how to let you know that I am so sorry that we lost touch. I heard about the death of your husband and I can't imagine how hard life has been for you. It is wonderful that this old war is finally over, and everyone can rebuild their lives the best they know how to. I hope we can too.

I am leaving Boston today for a thirty-day leave and will be home in Shawville over the holidays. It would be really nice for me if you could meet me at Mrs. Carlotta's on New Year's Eve, so we can get to know each other again. I understand if you would not want to or have other plans on such short notice, but please think about it to give me the chance I missed.

Thinking of you
Ross Kepple

Irene's heart skipped a beat after reading the letter from Ross. She could hardly believe it. She did write to Eddie to find out more about Ross but never heard back from him. There was no time to write back to Ross to let him know yes, she would be there and no, she didn't have other plans. She told her mom about the letter and Margaret was thrilled that Irene might have another chance at well-deserved happiness. The one-week wait was agony for Irene, but she used the time to get her hair cut and buy a new outfit and some fresh red lipstick.

# Chapter 38

New Year's Eve at Mrs. Carlotta's was always a festive event but in 1945 after the end of the war, it promised to be an enormous celebration.

The bar and the backroom were decorated with streamers hanging from the ceiling so thick you had to part them with your hands just to walk through the joint. Noisemakers were placed on every table as well as the bar and balloons were hanging everywhere.

Instead of relying on music from the jukebox, this night, Carlotta hired a live musical group to entertain the crowd. It was a trio of local men who played the piano, guitar and drums and they could sing anything from "Let Me Call You Sweetheart" to "God Bless America."

The party started early, and Ross strolled into the tavern around 8 o'clock and made his way through the streamers finding a seat around the u-shaped bar amidst many of his Shawville High School classmates shaking hands and hugging. The atmosphere was jovial as well as sad as they caught up with each other remembering those who were lost in the war. When the music began in the back room the fun began. Ross was careful not to drink too much and was nervous and anxious about possibly seeing Reeny again. He didn't know if she would show up. He didn't even know if she got his letter. He could only hope. It started snowing earlier in the day, typical for late December in Western Pennsylvania, and he hoped the roads would not get too bad tonight knowing if Reeny was coming she would have to drive about six miles to get there.

Reeny was nervous and anxious too as she carefully put on her new outfit, combed her hair and applied her new lipstick. She looked out the window to see a white blizzard of snow covering her Ford. She didn't know what exact time to be there but was pretty sure after midnight would be too late. Around 9 o'clock she kissed her mom, and 'the girls" goodbye and set out in the cold wintry night.

She could hardly see the road as she pulled out of her parking space and proceeded toward the old wooden bridge sliding all the way. Going very slow, Irene maneuvered the Ford onto the main road that led to Shawville. She had driven that road a hundred times before, but tonight it was almost impossible due to the weather, and out of the blue, the Ford slid off the road into a ditch on the side of road. She tried going forward and then backward to jar the car loose, but this just dug it in the ditch deeper and deeper. She was beside herself and didn't know what to do and started to cry.

Mrs. Carlotta's was jammed full and everyone was having a wonderful time dancing and singing and drinking. The townies could walk to the bar in spite of the weather, so the snow did not deter them. Ross kept looking out the window checking on the conditions outside when his friend, Ralph, said, "What are you worried about, you can walk home from here in this weather?"

This is when for the first time he let anyone know he was waiting for Reeny. "Ralph, do you remember Reeny, from a long time ago? You and Rose took us to a square dance at The Grange."

"Sure, I remember, she was a swell girl, what ever happened to her?"

"We lost touch during the war, but I was able to get her address and wrote to her. I invited her here tonight to meet me again, but I don't know if she will make it with all of this snow." Ross told him.

Irene decided sitting in the car and crying wasn't going to solve anything, so she grabbed her pocket book and wrapped a scarf around her head, got out of the car and started walking, walking toward Shawville. She was hoping someone would drive by and offer her a ride. That was her plan. She had no idea how long it would take her to get to Carlotta's, but she was on a mission.

It was nearing midnight and the countdown would begin soon. Ross was feeling defeated and a little drunk after realizing his expectation of meeting Reeny tonight were dwindling. He looked out the window one more time and decided she was not going to make it and had a shot and a beer. He walked into the backroom just in time to hear ten, nine, eight, seven, six, five, four, three, two, one...Happy New Year! The trio sang "Auld Lang Zang" and the crowd joined in raising their glasses in cheers.

Irene was about frozen to death walking along the road when finally, a single truck approached her. The driver shouted, "Where are you going, do you need a ride?"

She gratefully answered, "Oh yes, thank you, I am about frozen. I was trying to get to Mrs. Carlotta's in Shawville for the New Year's Eve party, but my car got stuck in a ditch."

The driver responded, "Well, I just came from there and the party is over, but I can take you there to get warmed up. I think they will be open for another hour or so." Irene climbed into the passenger side, thanking him as he turned up the heat to help thaw her out.

He dropped her off along the main hill and she walked into Carlotta's looking distraught and exhausted. She scanned the room looking for any sign of Ross, but instead she saw the remains of a party that she missed with streamers on the floor and the trio packing up their equipment. She sat down at one of the tables when Mrs. Carlotta came into the room from the swinging doors that led to the bar and said, "Honey, it's almost closing time, but you can have last call if you want."

Irene said, "Yes, please get me a beer, and can I ask you a favor?"

"Sure, what can I do for you?"

"Can you turn on the jukebox, so I can play one song?"

Mrs. Carlotta turned it on and said, "The song is on us, Happy New Year."

Irene grabbed the beer bottle and took a long drink and walked over to the jukebox. She scanned the menu and soon found "Marie". She punched the numbers and the song began to play.

Ross was just about to leave and walk home, after one more beer, when he heard the music from the backroom. He recognized the song, it was "Marie". He pushed his way through the swinging doors and walked over to the woman who had her back to him looking at the jukebox. He said, "Reeny, it's you."

She turned around and looked into his sky-blue eyes and said, "Yes Ross it's me." They embraced and kissed, and Ross wiped tears from her eyes and pushed her hair off her face. "I thought I missed you and got here too late." She began to explain.

He just said, "Shhh, everything is alright now." and they swayed to the song holding each other tight knowing everything was going to be alright.

# Epilogue

Since I began writing this story after reading the letters in that old satchel, much has changed regarding Mom and her stay at the Shawville Medical Center. Her disease progressed, and she got weaker and required more medical procedures, just to keep her alive.

What bothered me the most was that she hated being there, and as hard as I tried to keep her spirits up, she still just wanted to go home.

Grace and Shirley were life savers for me. They visited as often as they could, bringing mom snacks and painting her nails, arranging for hair appointments and whatever else they could think of to take care of their older sister who took such good care of them when they needed it. "The girls" loved her.

I would take Dad to visit with Mom when he felt up to it, but these visits became less frequent as time went on.

Dad's declining health and his situation at home eventually forced me to arrange for him to become a resident of the Shawville Medical Center too. It became evident that my brother and his wife could no longer take care of him, as promised.

I was excited the day I went to mom's room to tell her the good news. "Hi Mom," I said. She was sitting in her wheelchair, leaning to the left, even though she was propped up with pillows, looking a little disoriented.

"Hi Marie," she said smiling. "I'm so glad to see you." I leaned down and gave her a kiss on the cheek and sat on the edge of her bed next to her.

"I have news for you mom, dad is staying here now too." I said.

She got a bewildered look on her face and said, "What did you say?"

I said, "Dad is here at the Medical Center too, now you too can see each other every day." To my surprise, mom began to cry. I said, "What is wrong, why are you crying?"

In between her sobs, she said, "Now I will never get to go home. If Ross was still there, I had hope that he would bring me back to our home. Now there is no hope."

After a while she accepted the situation and was glad to see Dad much more often than before.

Then I got the call I knew would come someday. My phone rang at 9 a.m. on December 20. I will never forget the exact words. "Marie, this is Susan from the Medical Center. Your mom woke up this morning and then she stopped breathing."

The ringing phone had woken me up and I was still half asleep. I groggily said, "Yes", expecting her to say that she came around and everything was alright, but that is not what she said.

"She's gone," were the next words I heard.

It took me a while to focus on what I just heard and when I did, I said "I will be right up." I woke my husband and said, "Mom died."

I immediately called Shirley and told her and she in turn called Grace and the three of us made our way to the Shawville Medical Center.

Once I got there and paid respects to Mom, my next arduous task was to tell Dad. Shirley accompanied me to Dad's room and after the usual greetings, I said, "I have some bad news, Mom passed away this morning."

Dad, being hard of hearing said, "What?" So, after repeating that mom had died, we all burst into tears. After he composed himself he said, "I guess everybody has to die, we always wondered who would go first."

Arrangements were made, relatives were called, and the funeral was held on December 23. It was almost Christmas. She was 83 years old.

Dad also passed away while a resident of the Medical Center three years later on March 6. He was 87 years old.

Reeny and Ross got married on April 8, 1947 after he served his six years in the Navy. They bought a house in Shawville with the money Irene had put under the mattress from Merle's insurance policy from the government. They were married for 57 years, had four kids and eight grandsons. They lived life to the fullest and were the happiest with their family, especially those eight grandsons.

So that is the end of my story. I am very
grateful that I was fortunate enough to obtain the
letters from the attic and able to memorialize the
lives of these three people during this
unforgettable moment in our history. I know there
are many stories documenting these years, but
this is my story.

**The End**

Made in the USA
Middletown, DE
01 July 2018